"Am I so frightening?" Vin asked her

"Not today," Tansy confessed. "But you can be somewhat aloof."

"Frequently it's a man's way of resisting a beautiful woman."

Did this mean he was no longer trying to resist her? And did he really find her beautiful?

Convinced he was flirting with her, Tansy wasn't sure how to react. In normal circumstances his comments wouldn't have been a problem, but their working relationship changed that. Besides, he was a damnably attractive man and she could easily fall for him.

"No comments, Tansy?"

"No comments."

"One day," he said, "I won't allow you to play it safe."

ROBERTA LEIGH wrote her first book at the age of nineteen and since then has written more than seventy romance novels, as well as many books and film series for children. She has also been an editor of a woman's magazine and produced a teen magazine, but writing romance fiction remains one of her greatest joys. She lives in Hampstead, London, and has one son.

Books by Roberta Leigh

ROBERTA LEIGH

one girl at a time

Harlequin Books

TORONTO • NEW YORK • LONDON
AMSTERDAM • PARIS • SYDNEY • HAMBURG
STOCKHOLM • ATHENS • TOKYO • MILAN

Harlequin Presents first edition December 1991
ISBN 0-373-11420-6

Original hardcover edition published in 1990
by Mills & Boon Limited

ONE GIRL AT A TIME

CHAPTER ONE

TANSY sank her feet into the soft white sand, stared at the shimmering turquoise-blue sea and flung her arms wide. It was incredible that she was here in Thailand!

Ten days in Hua Hin—one of the country's oldest resorts—lay behind her, with two more in Bangkok ahead, and she refused to be depressed by the possibility of closing her dress business on her return to London.

Her worries had started with her sister Sara's car accident and four months' coma. Though Tansy didn't regret the daily vigil at her bedside, it meant she had missed her last term at fashion college, and the chance to show her designs to the manufacturers who flocked to the graduation show. But her compensation had been the joy of her sister's recovery, due in part to John Fenton, the doctor who first met Sara as his patient, and subsequently made her his wife.

It was because of John that Tansy was here, for when she had collapsed with flu and taken months to recover he had presented her with this trip.

'Unfortunately we can't afford to help you get on your feet professionally,' he had said, 'but when you're physically fit you'll be better able to cope.'

Gratefully Tansy had accepted their gift, forbearing to say health alone wasn't enough to save her business. For that, she required sufficient money to make at least a dozen different samples, for no one would bother coming to see less.

Sighing away her despondency, she meandered across the sand to where several fishing boats were beached, and watched straw-hatted women haggling over the price of the fish and crustaceans being unloaded.

'What sensational hair!' a male American voice exclaimed.

Tansy, used to hearing such comments on her riotous curls, refused to look round.

'It's pure Titian red,' the voice went on.

At least he'd heard of the Italian Master! Glancing round, she saw a blond giant of a man with a bushy beard. Disreputable shorts and shirt covered his body, and what little of his face wasn't masked by beard was hidden by a dilapidated sun-hat.

She moved off, irritated when he followed her. She was here to recuperate, not start a holiday flirtation. Come to think of it, flirting had never interested her, anyway. Her number one priority had always been her career.

'Staying here long?' the man behind her asked.

She didn't turn. 'I'm leaving for Bangkok today.'

'So am I. If you care to ride pillion, I'll give you a lift on my motorbike.'

'No, thanks, I've too much luggage.' She quickened her pace, and so did he.

'How long will you be in Bangkok?' he asked.

'Two days.'

'Perhaps we——'

'Sorry, I'll be busy.'

She headed towards a nearby *samlor* rank. They were similar to the rickshaws found in parts of Asia and India, except these weren't pulled by people but fixed to a tricycle and pedalled by the driver.

'How much to the Royal Garden hotel?' she asked the boy on the seat.

'Forty *baht*.'

This was almost a pound and she shook her head. 'Fifteen.'

'Thirty.'

With a shrug she walked off, a trick she had learned from her fellow guests at the hotel.

'OK, sir!' the boy called. 'Fifteen.'

Straight-faced, she clambered into the rickety vehicle, holding on to her sun-hat as her enthusiastic driver—standing upright on the pedals—manoeuvred his way through the traffic.

Ten minutes later Tansy was in her bedroom packing, and four hours afterwards was unpacking in the Royal Orchid in Bangkok. Though not in the super-luxury class of the Oriental or Shangri-La, it was luxurious to Tansy, and through the picture window she enjoyed a superb view of the Chao Phraya River seven storeys below.

Although her dress was crumpled she was reluctant to waste time changing it and, running a comb through her unruly curls, set off to explore the city.

The foyer was crowded, and as she walked towards the entrance she noticed a sign saying 'River City Shopping Mall, First Floor'. She stopped in her tracks, torn between a desire to sightsee and her instincts as a designer. The designer won—after all, she was booked for a day-long tour tomorrow—and she went up to the first floor and through a glass enclosed walkway to a large, modern shopping complex. It sold the expected tourist attractions, from snakeskin bags and shoes, to jewellery, antiques and wood carvings. Predictably, many shops were given over to Thai silk, available by the metre or made up into clothes.

The materials were beautiful but the styling disappointing, and she ambled from one store to another until she rounded a corner and saw two large windows, one filled with bolts of silk, the other with dresses. 'Arunila' was the gilded name above the door, and with hope revived Tansy went in.

She should have saved herself the trouble! The clothes here were the worst, and as she went to walk out a dainty Thai girl glided up to her.

'I help you, please?'

'I think I could be of more help to *you*,' Tansy couldn't resist answering, pointing to a zip on a dress. 'This is so heavy it could be used on a shopping bag!'

'But our silk is beautiful.'

'I agree, but the styles have come out of the ark!'

'No one is forcing you to buy here.'

A sarcastic masculine voice spoke behind Tansy, and she wheeled round to find herself being surveyed by a tall, spare man wearing rimmed black sunglasses. How weird to be wearing them indoors, she reflected, though the rest of him wasn't weird at all. Indeed, with his straight black hair, olive skin and narrow-boned face, he could have passed for a Spaniard. But his murmured aside to the assistant showed him to be Thai, and Tansy wished she knew what he had said.

'You are welcome to look round without buying,' the man addressed her again, his English holding barely a trace of an accent, his tone as steely as the muscles beneath his pale grey suit. 'But it is impolite to criticise the clothes so other customers can hear you.'

Tansy knew she deserved the reprimand, and had the man not acted as if she were a worm that had crawled out of the cheese she would have apologised. But he was the rudest person she had encountered in Thailand. His height—around six feet—and his fine-cut features proclaimed him a northerner, and she wondered if they were less friendly than their southern compatriots.

'It may have been impolite of me,' she said in her haughtiest voice, 'but I was so astonished by the poor quality that I——'

'You consider yourself a judge?' The movement of his head took in her crumpled dress, and she wished she had taken time to change it.

'I certainly do. London stores buy everything I design and make.' Upon which comment she stalked out.

She was still seething when she returned to her hotel, and the first person she saw towering over everyone else was the bushy-bearded hippy who had tried to chat her up on the beach at Hua Hin. At least he had left off his outrageous hat, and she saw his hair was blond and wavy, and his face—the part not covered by fungus—was fresh-complexioned.

His sherry-brown eyes lit up at sight of her, and he loped over to her as though they had parted the best of friends. Despite herself, Tansy smiled at him.

'What a stroke of luck bumping into you!' he exclaimed.

'I gave you the brush-off yesterday.'

'But you gave me a smile today, so you must be regretting it!'

'I wouldn't go as far as that.'

'Would you go as far as having dinner with me?'

Flummoxed, she hesitated.

'Be a devil and say yes. I swear I'm not as disreputable as I appear.'

'I'm glad to hear it.'

'Does that mean yes?' He held out his hand. 'I'm Kevin Jay.'

'Tansy Simmonds,' she replied. 'When and where shall we meet?'

'Here at eight.' His eyes went to her hair. 'Fantastic,' he breathed, and loped off.

Almost at once Tansy regretted accepting the invitation, then chided herself for being antisocial; dinner with an extrovert hippy was less boring than eating alone.

After a leisurely bath she changed into one of her own creations: a voile dress with an overall pattern of greens, blues and lilac. Pleated from neck to hem, it was deceptively simple but showed her tall, slender body to advantage, its colours emphasising the flaming curls cascading around her face and down her back.

Bracing herself for another of Kevin's compliments, she went to meet him, so startled by his appearance that she stopped dead. His beard and hair were combed smooth, and his frayed shorts and shirt were replaced by well-cut navy trousers and blue jacket.

'What a handsome couple we are!' he joked. 'I'm glad I booked a table at the Oriental Hotel.'

'Isn't that very expensive?'

'Isn't it rude of you to comment?' he mocked.

'Probably. But I don't want you wasting your money on me. I'm happy to eat at the food stalls. I hear they're excellent.'

'They are. But tonight we're going somewhere special.'

'Then we'll go Dutch.'

'We'll go American—which means I'll pay!' He steered her out to a taxi. 'But thanks for the offer. You're nice as well as beautiful.'

Tansy giggled, suddenly feeling young and carefree, which was a mood she hadn't experienced for far too long.

The Oriental prided itself on its dignified luxuriousness. Other hotels were bigger and more lavish, but none had the regality, the same air of confidence in its service.

With equal confidence Kevin escorted Tansy across the vast coolness of the marble reception hall, to an excellent table overlooking the Chao Phraya River.

'I hope you like barbecues?' he asked when they were seated.

'Love 'em.'

Her eyes moved from the river—its darkness relieved by the glow of river buses—to the dozen or so large barbecue carts, their embers bright, which ranged along the terrace. Each was tended by a chef, and people milled round them, piling their plates with seafood or exotic curries redolent of lemon grass, coconut, mouth-burning chillies and Eastern spices.

'Let's have a drink first,' Kevin suggested. 'Fancy a Pina Colada?'

'What's that?'

'Wait and see.' He stopped a passing waiter, and within a few moments two tall glasses of milky fluid were set before them. 'To us!' Kevin toasted, raising his glass.

'Cheers!' Tansy responded, deeming it safer to offer a more prosaic toast. Gingerly she sipped. 'Mmm, delicious. Like a coconut milk shake.'

'Alcoholic too.' Kevin's eyes twinkled as she hastily set down her glass. 'I only said it to warn you!'

Smiling, she took another sip. 'Ever had coconut milk direct from the nut?'

'Often. I've even shinned up a tree and picked my own.'

'You sound a seasoned traveller.'

'I've wandered around for two years. I only work when I need money! Then I teach English.'

Tansy's sapphire-blue eyes crinkled. 'I didn't take you for a teacher.'

'I'm not—by profession. I simply help anyone who wants to learn it. I've been teaching a couple and their five kids in Hua Hin the last four months. Now I'm off to Malaysia. But enough about me. What do *you* do?'

'I design and make clothes—though I may soon have to use the past tense.'

'Hard going?'

'Ever tried eating peas with a pin?' Briefly she recounted her tale of woe.

'You'd be wiser cutting your losses and taking a job with someone else,' he commented as she finished.

'Designing what a dress manufacturer wants?' Tansy's curls bounced as she shook her head. 'I'd rather scrub floors—and I may have to——!'

She broke off as there was a flurry behind Kevin, and the *maître d'hôtel* hurried to greet a couple coming towards him. Surely the fuss wasn't on account of the leggy blonde? Granted she was beautiful, but so were many other women here. The man with her—talking to someone behind him so Tansy only glimpsed his back—was a different story. Tall, slim, with wide shoulders and jet-black hair, he was—jeepers!

It was the boorish Thai from the dress shop—and still sporting those black sunglasses!

'Anyone you know?' Kevin enquired as he heard her gasp.

'Yes, the man.' From the corner of her eye she watched the couple being escorted to the table behind Kevin, which brought the Thai directly in her line of vision. Surreptitiously she shifted her chair.

'I take it you'd rather he doesn't see you?' Kevin remarked humorously, and shamefacedly she confessed the reason, which had him choking with laughter. 'No wonder he didn't take to you. You're the kind of customer no one needs!'

'If the silly man hadn't provoked me, I'd have apologised. But he was so supercilious I saw red.'

'I guess you're a fiery lady when roused.' Kevin shot a quick glance behind him. 'I'm afraid we'll have to pass his table on the way to the barbecue.'

'So what? He won't bite me.'

'More likely the other way round!' Kevin rejoined, rising and drawing her to her feet.

She clung to his arm as if she had eyes for no one else, and because of it passed so close to the Thai's table that her dress brushed his trouser-leg. Instantly her eyes went to him, meeting the flash of black lenses. Darn him for coming here! With hundreds of restaurants to choose from, what bad luck they should be at the same one.

Reaching the barbecue carts, she soon forgot everything except the mouth-watering displays in front of her. Accepting Kevin's guidance, she chose chicken soup flavoured with lemon grass and coconut milk, and a mild beef curry.

'Have some seafood too,' he urged. 'It's fantastic in Thailand.'

Conscious of cost, she declined.

'Be a devil. It's a barbecue and there's an all-in price regardless of how much you stuff yourself!'

'Then I'll have a lobster and some of those huge tiger prawns.'

Kevin tapped her cheek. 'Are you always so worried by what your date's spending?'

'Well . . . I don't know you and——'

'I can afford it. Living in a small village for months, I've had nothing on which to spend my money.'

Plates filled, they returned to their table, but throughout the meal Tansy was mindful of the Thai at the next one, and the flash of black glass as he occasionally leaned towards the blonde, or tipped back his head to laugh at something she said.

'I'm ready for seconds,' Kevin announced, pushing back his chair. 'How about you?'

Declining, Tansy remained where she was, and, under the pretext of studying her surroundings, glanced at the man whose presence had disturbed her all evening. The girl with him interested her too. A typical Nordic beauty, with a swathe of long, blonde hair caught back with a pair of jewelled combs, she reeked of pampered indolence.

If only I had hair like hers, Tansy mused, instead of curls with a life of their own! Watching, she saw the blonde place a scarlet-tipped hand on the man's cheek. Would a wife make such a public gesture of affection? She doubted it, and ironically concluded the girl was a very close friend.

Glad they were too engrossed in each other to be aware of her, Tansy focused on the man. His wrap-around spectacles obscured not only his eyes but part of his nose, making it difficult to assess his looks, though they didn't hide the narrow, flaring nostrils and fine-cut mouth, nor the smile that would tug at most girls' heart-strings. He was in a dark suit to-night, its impeccable cut drawing attention to the whipcord leanness of his body.

As she watched, the man and girl rose, his arm lightly touching her waist. What a figure she had! She was greyhound-slim yet full-breasted, her scarlet sheath showed every curve, while the provocative slit up the side revealed a shapely leg. One thing was for sure, Tansy concluded—that dress didn't come from the shop her escort managed!

'You'd think I hadn't eaten for days!'

It was Kevin again, and Tansy forced a smile, then darted her eyes to the couple, relieved as a waiter cleared their table. Now she could concentrate on Kevin, she thought contritely. He deserved better than an inattentive dinner companion.

It was shortly after eleven when they rose to leave, and as they crossed the lobby someone called his name. He stopped abruptly, staring with pleasure at another blond giant by the reception desk.

'If it isn't Chuck!' He glanced at Tansy. 'I haven't seen him since college. Come and meet him.'

'I won't, if you don't mind,' she murmured. 'The air-conditioning's cold and I'll wait outside and warm up!'

Leaving him bounding towards his mirror image, Tansy headed for the entrance, hesitating as she saw the willowy blond standing there alone, as if waiting.

Head averted, she slipped outside and stood as far away from the doors as possible. The last thing she fancied was encountering the supercilious Thai as he came out. She wandered to the edge of the kerb, jumping back with a cry as a white Porsche screeched to a stop alongside her, and the demon king himself unfolded long legs and emerged.

Heavens! This wasn't her day. Nor his, it appeared, the way he scowled at her.

'I could have hit you,' he snarled.

'You shouldn't drive so fast near a hotel entrance.'

The briefest nod acknowledged this. 'Are you always bad-tempered?'

'Only when I encounter bad manners!'

'From your behaviour earlier today, you're an excellent judge of those! You are the rudest young woman I've met.'

'And you are the most pompous man!'

His sardonic smile, showing very white teeth, disclaimed her opinion, and without a word he strode over to the elegant silver-blonde who was undulating towards him, and helped her into the car.

Thank goodness he's gone, Tansy thought as they drove away. If she was ever unfortunate enough to meet him again, she would cut him dead!

CHAPTER TWO

Two days later, Tansy was back in her modest workroom-cum-apartment in the centre of the garment district in London.

Depression settled over her as she gazed at the bolts of material and the pristine cutting table, and despite being jet-lagged she settled herself by the telephone and began calling every customer she had ever supplied.

By noon her orders still barely covered her expenses for two weeks, and she ruefully conceded it was stupid to carry on like this. Better to face reality and find a job with a dress manufacturer—as Kevin had said. It would at least give her a decent wage and enable her to start repaying the money she owed her parents, who had helped her get started.

Or should she do the garments she had talked her guts out to get, and see if anything else materialised meantime? Hell! She was like Mr Micawber, hoping something would turn up to save her.

Frowning, she put on the kettle, and was taking her first sip of tea when Diana Gray, her favourite tutor at fashion college, called her.

'How are things going with you, Tansy?'

'Not too badly.'

'Which means they're awful, but you're too proud to ask me for help!'

Tansy's throat thickened with tears. 'I'm not a student any longer. I can't come running to you for help.'

'Why not?'

Tansy hesitated. 'I knew you were upset with me for not completing my garments for the graduation show, and——'

'I was wrong and I apologise. If I hadn't been convinced you'd take first prize, I'd have been more understanding.' The woman paused. 'You must be busy making samples for next summer, so pick out six of your best and——'

'I haven't started thinking of summer yet!'

'Then start doing so now. I want them by the end of the month.'

Tansy bit back a sigh, too proud to admit she could not afford to buy the materials and trimmings necessary to do as her ex-tutor requested. Yet to refuse . . .

'Is it all right if I do them in cotton?'

'Don't be silly. I want a suit, three day dresses, and two for evening, and——' Mrs Gray's voice rose in apology. 'Oh, my dear, how stupid of me. Go to Brown and Franks and charge everything to my account. Don't worry about cost. You can repay me when you have the contract.'

'What contract?'

'Didn't I tell you? A cash-rich firm is shopping for a designer, and asked me to suggest the best ones I know. So get cracking.'

For the next few days Tansy sketched and discarded until she had six inspired designs. Only then did she take up the tutor's offer to subsidise the cost of the materials, and twenty back-breaking, bent-over-the-sewing-room-table days later, she delivered the complete outfits.

Waiting for news was two weeks of nail-biting tension, and she was in the trough of pessimism when Mrs Gray marched into her workroom, face alight.

'You've got the job!' she announced. 'Mr Makram saw thirty designers worldwide, and considered you the best.'

Tansy hugged the woman close. 'I can't believe it! It's a dream come true.'

'Your dream's just beginning. Apart from this dress company, Mr Makram owns one of the largest property empires in the Far East, and has the financial muscle to give you all the help you need.'

'You mean the factory isn't in England?'

'That's right. It was the original family business. From what he told me, he'd have preferred closing it, but his father started Arunila twenty-five years ago and is very sentimental about it.'

'Arunila?' Tansy's mouth fell open! 'Oh, lord!'

'You know it?'

'I'll say!' Succinctly she related what had happened in Bangkok.

'You should be tickled pink you've won the contract,' Diana Gray informed her. 'I'd like to be a fly on the wall when you make that manager eat his words! Just imagine!'

Tansy did, and felt better for it. 'What will I actually have to do for the company?'

'Design three collections a year. A winter and a summer one for Europe and the Americas, and a beachwear one for the December-to-April tourist season in Thailand, which will also be sold in Australasia. You'll be expected to oversee the production of the samples that will be shown to the buyers, but once they've placed their orders the factory will take over.'

Tansy glanced round her tiny workroom. 'I'll have to move to larger premises.'

'My dear girl, you'll be expected to move to Thailand!'

'Oh!'

'What's to "oh" about? This is your big chance. The clothes will be distributed in Europe and the States by Impo, a top firm, and my guess is that a year from now you'll be a name to be reckoned with.'

Opening her purse, the tutor handed Tansy a four-page contract. It was for five years' duration and gave Arunila the right to break it if they did not like her first collection, or if it proved to be a failure, when she would be given a year's salary and all out-of-pocket expenses.

'Mr Makram had to go to Hong Kong urgently, and apologises for not seeing you himself. But I had a long talk with him and found him eminently fair-minded. Sign with him, Tansy, you've nothing to lose except your debts!'

Six weeks to the day, Tansy arrived in Chiang Mai, an hour's flight north of Bangkok, where the Arunila factories were. A chauffeur-driven limousine took her through the small town which, despite the noise of thousands of motorcycles and tuk-tuks—motorised rickshaws, according to her startled eyes—was far more picturesque than the capital, with its backdrop of lush-covered mountains.

She had been booked into the Rincome, a modern yet traditional hotel which stood at the foot of Doi Suthep mountain, yet was within easy reach of the main shopping centre. Glistening white outside, its interior was a mix of bamboo and teakwood furniture, with a plethora of small elephant statues.

Tired from her long journey, she was leisurely unpacking when a bellboy delivered a basket of mauve orchids. The card attached held a handwritten message from Mr Makram, welcoming her and saying he looked forward to meeting her at his office at two o'clock the following afternoon. Pleased she had a day to acclimatise, she decided to meander round the town before having an early dinner and a long night's sleep.

An hour later, changed into a lemon cotton shift, she went into the Lanna Coffee Shop for a snack. Its dark floor and furniture was offset by the colourful sunshades hanging open from the ceiling. Some were made in cotton or silk, but most were in sa-paper which—her smiling waitress informed her—came from the bark of the mulberry tree.

Craning her neck, Tansy studied the designs, which were pretty enough to be used as motifs on a selection of beach wear. She half smiled, knowing she'd have— and discard—many such ideas before she finally sat at her drawing-board.

Picking up the menu, she scanned it, then settled for a prawn salad. It came with a side portion of Thai rice, white and glutinous and much favoured here, as it was excellent for absorbing the delicious sauces which were an integral part of their cuisine.

Afterwards, refreshed by a strong coffee, she wandered the streets, breathing deeply of the glorious champagne air. Although late October, and the hot season didn't officially start until March, it was warm as a lovely English summer's day, the air clear enough to see the variegated greens of the wooded, mountainous landscapes.

Her eye was drawn to Doi Suthep, the nearest one, and the Buddhist temple shining at the very top. She longed to climb the zig-zag road to it but knew this had to come low on her agenda. First was to meet Mr Makram and find out exactly what was wanted of her.

To fill in the rest of the day she toured the town, viewing the stone walls surrounding the older part of it, wandering along the bank of the Ping River which bisected it, and gaining a feeling of its ancient past, when this province had been a country of its own ruled by a king.

Exploring the shops, some no bigger than a small room, she was amazed by the lacquerware, hand-beaten silver, wood carvings and silks, and naturally lingered longest over the materials, noticing many unusual patterns.

'Designs come from hill tribes,' a salesgirl replied in answer to Tansy's question. 'If wish see, go higher north where silk made by hand.'

Restraining the urge to rush there, Tansy returned to the hotel. It was dusk and considerably cooler, and she was sorry she hadn't worn a cardigan. A warm bath restored her circulation, and she changed into a wool dress before going down to dinner.

Anxious to be at her best for tomorrow's meeting, she avoided the spicier dishes in case they upset her, settling for papaw, and chicken wings in red wine sauce, which had no wine in it, but was undoubtedly red!

Nine-thirty found her in her room again, and, disregarding her biological clock which was out of true with local time, she went to bed. Convinced she wouldn't sleep for hours, she did so almost as her head touched the pillow, and awoke with a horrified start to find bright sunlight streaming into her room. Heavens, she'd missed her appointment!

A glance at her watch showed it was only eight-thirty, and with a sigh of relief she pushed aside the blankets and padded over to the window. Sight of the town spread out in front of her gave her a warm, friendly feeling, and intuitively she knew she was going to like it here—provided things went well with Arunila!

The fear that they mightn't gave her a pang of disquiet, and unwilling to brood she went to have breakfast, discovering the croissants to be as good as any she had had in France.

Afterwards she took a stroll, upbraiding herself for being nervous. This was her big break, and she had to convince Mr Makram she was capable of making his dress company a force to be reckoned with.

She reminded herself of this when she entered the offices of Land Incorporated, which was also the headquarters of Arunila Silks. It was in one of the newest buildings in Chiang Mai, the regulation four storeys high, and as modern inside as out, with teak desks, black leather chairs, and a proliferation of flowering plants.

Giving her name to a uniformed porter, she was escorted to the top floor and an air-conditioned reception area, where a Thai girl in a cheongsam—a tight-fitting skirt with a slit in the side to make walking easier, and a figure-hugging jacket with high, round neck and long tight sleeves—took her name and asked her to wait.

After a few minutes, another girl appeared and escorted her along a carpeted corridor to a door at the end.

Tansy found herself in a very large room, her first nervous glance showing her beige, silk-covered walls, numerous Chinese paintings—black lines and muted pastels—and a vast glass-topped desk behind which was an imposing black leather chair.

But it was the figure rising from it who brought her heart into her mouth.

It couldn't be! Life wasn't so cruel. Yet it was, and not just cruel, but diabolical, for the spare-framed, wide-shouldered man whose face was turned to her with equal disbelief was the manager of the Arunila shop in Bangkok! Whoever had said third time lucky should be hung, drawn and quartered!

He was still wearing wrap-around spectacles, their Stygian lenses completely masking his eyes. But his dismay was apparent from the flare of his nostrils and the thinning of his mouth.

'*You* are Miss Simmonds?' His voice dripped ice.

'I'm as surprised as you are.' She marvelled she could speak. 'If I'd known...'

Silently he sat down, motioning her to do the same, and she took a straight-back chair in front of his desk, resisting the impulse to take one near the door.

She had signed a contract and they were stuck with one another unless it was possible for him to break it by citing their previous meeting. Thinking of her ambitious plans for her future, she almost wept.

'It's regrettable we weren't able to meet in London,' he said. 'But, even if we had, I'd have made the same decision.' Noting her expression, the faintest smile lifted the edge of his mouth. 'I'm a pragmatist, Miss

Simmonds, and I don't cut off my nose to spite my face. I chose you because your work was outstanding, and as you once rightly, if impolitely informed me, we urgently require to improve our image. So I suggest we put our previous unpleasant encounters behind us, and pull together for the success of the company.'

Speechlessly Tansy heard him out, wishing she could see if his eyes mirrored his calm, businesslike manner. He was a picture of quiet confidence: slim-fingered hands resting on his desk, glossy black hair brushed smoothly away from a high forehead, mouth slightly quirked, showing that when it wasn't compressed with anger it was beautifully shaped, with a full lower lip.

'Well?' he asked, steel beneath the velvet tone.

'I agree.' Her voice was equally steely, and, making sure her skirt didn't rise above her knees, she settled back into the chair, hoping to give an impression of ease.

'You seem different from the first time we met,' he stated, the slight movement of his head indicating his appraisal of her. 'If it weren't for your hair, I wouldn't have recognised you.'

'Most people remember red hair.'

'More the colour of claret, Miss Simmonds—my favourite drink.'

Goodness, he had actually made a joke! Or had he? Regarding his expressionless face, she wasn't sure, and deemed it wiser to let it pass.

'I'd like to know the exact market you are aiming for, Mr Makram, as well as the price range.'

'Expensive enough to be relatively exclusive, but not the crazy prices of couture.'

'Some ready-to-wear can cost upwards of two thousand pounds a dress. Is that what you have in mind?'

'No, half that.'

'Very well. Before I start designing I'd like to see the materials you produce, and the factory where the garments are made.'

'That's easily arranged. When you've done so, let me know what you think. And don't worry about being tactful.' His head tilted. 'If memory serves me right, I suppose it wasn't necessary for me to say that!'

She swallowed a sharp retort. 'I'm afraid I don't speak Thai,' she said instead, 'and I may have to ask some pertinent questions.'

'I've assigned an assistant to you.' He paused. 'How soon will you get back to me?'

'Not later than a week. I also intend visiting the firms who supply your trimmings.'

'Ah, yes, you objected to our zips!'

'And buttons and belts!'

'All the trimmings come from Bangkok.'

'I'll go there and see if they can do better. If not, we'll have to order them from France or Italy.'

'Is that necessary?'

'Yes.' It took an effort for Tansy to speak calmly. 'I don't spend money for the sake of it, Mr Makram.'

'I'm not setting you a limit.' His quiet tone showed his awareness of her annoyance. 'I am quite happy to accept Mrs Gray's word that you are both creative and financially responsible.'

Tansy nodded, and was on the verge of rising when a sweet-faced Thai girl came in and handed him a sheaf of documents. They entered into a spirited conversation and she was sorry she couldn't follow it, for the friendliness between them made her wonder about their relationship, a curiosity which increased when the girl suddenly spoke in English.

'Will that be all, Vin?'

'Yes, until I've gone over the papers.'

As the girl went out, Tansy glanced at Mr Makram and found him watching her with a humorous expression that not even his enveloping glasses could hide.

'Renaud is my secretary, Miss Simmonds. Nothing more.'

'I didn't say——'

'Your eyes did it for you!' One long-fingered hand toyed with a slim gold fountain pen. 'I'm curious to know why you assumed it.'

He had asked for the truth and Tansy resolved to give it to him. 'She called you by your first name, and you don't strike me as the sort of employer who'd go for that.'

'It isn't our custom to use surnames.'

'I see.' Deflated, she fell silent.

'It doesn't apply when we speak to foreigners,' he added. 'So you needn't be afraid I'll encourage you to an intimacy you would clearly find embarrassing.'

What a boorish pig he was! Did she come across as so uptight that he thought she'd object to being called Tansy, or be unwilling to call him Vin? Suddenly she longed for the freedom of being her own boss, and was devastated to think she was thousands of miles from home and family.

'You may find things strange here at first,' he said into the silence, 'but we'll do our best to make you welcome.'

She relaxed, and was thinking he wasn't as bad as she had supposed when he confounded her by saying, 'Of course you understand that if we don't like your first collection we can dispense with your services?'

'Yes.'

'Naturally you'd receive compensation.'

'I know that too. It's in our agreement.' She wasn't going to let him think she'd have relied on his good nature! 'But no money would compensate me for having to return home with my tail between my legs! I left a lucrative business to come here.'

'None the less you agreed to do it.'

Tansy resisted the urge to hit him, glad when another tap at the door heralded the entry of a man in his late twenties. Unlike Mr Makram, who was considerably taller than the average Thai male, he was about five feet seven, and darker-skinned. He was thin but wiry, his face was high-cheekboned, with almond-shaped brown eyes, a small nose, and a wide mouth showing extremely white teeth when he smiled, which he was now doing at her.

'Deng, this is Miss Simmonds.' Mr Makram's dark glasses flashed in her direction. 'Deng will be your personal assistant.'

'It's a pleasure meeting you,' Deng beamed, his English as good as his employer's, though with a pronounced American accent.

'Miss Simmonds wishes to see how our factories operate,' Mr Makram went on, 'and I have assured her you will give her every help.'

His tone made it clear the meeting was over, and Tansy went to the door, the younger man at her side. She was on the threshold when Mr Makram spoke again.

'Deng will drive you wherever you wish to go, but if you care to drive yourself I will arrange for you to have a car.'

'Thank you for the offer, but I don't drive.'

Smiling goodbye again, she went out, wishing she had never signed this contract, had never come to Thailand, and had never met the overbearing, confident, and supercilious man who was now her boss.

CHAPTER THREE

'IT WILL be better if you look at our factories tomorrow morning,' Deng said as he accompanied her to the ground floor, and Tansy, assuming their hours were the same as British ones, nodded.

'Are they in Chiang Mai?' she asked.

'No, in San Kamphaeng, a small town east of here. It's where most of the silk industry is. If it's OK with you, I'll pick you up at eight-thirty in the morning.'

Expecting him to say goodbye at the entrance, she was gratified when he led her to a blue Toyota parked by the kerb. 'There's no need for you to take me to the hotel,' she protested.

'It's my pleasure. Besides, I'd like to know more about you.'

Recollecting that friendly curiosity was a Thai characteristic, and that it wasn't considered impolite to ask intimate questions, she gave him a brief, rose-spectacled version of her working life to date.

'As a student I thought I'd get to the top in a couple of years,' she concluded. 'But I now know it takes more than talent and hard work. Without luck, it's like trying to skate in slippers!'

'Your luck began when you signed with Khun Vin.'

'With who?'

'Ha! You don't know our custom with names,' Deng grinned. 'When we speak or refer to anyone, we always use their first name. But as a mark of respect we put *Khun* in front of it. It means Mr, Mrs or Miss.'

'You call *everyone* by their first name?'

'Sure. But as you're a *farang*—a foreigner—he won't think it strange if you call him Mr Makram. Another thing to remember is that married women aren't called by their husband's surname either, so there'd never be a Mrs Makram.'

'What would she be called then?'

'Either Khun Vin—which means Mrs Vin—or Khun plus her first name.'

Waspishly, Tansy felt sorry for the poor girl married to him. 'When I was in Bangkok a few months ago I saw Mr Makram with his wife.'

'Not possible. He's single, though plenty of women have set their sights at him. But so far he's eluded capture!'

Remembering the blonde and the red-tipped hand that had caressed Mr Makram's cheek, Tansy felt foolish and hurriedly said, 'Have *you* been captured yet?'

'I'm too crafty!'

She laughed. 'Your English is very idiomatic. Did you learn it here?'

'No. I worked for an uncle in California for five years. He manufactures sportswear and trained me as a designer.'

'What brought you back here?'

'I missed my country.' Deng slowed at the traffic lights. 'One morning I read an article about Khun Vin, and when I learned he was in San Francisco I arranged to see him. I was hoping he'd let me design for him, but he asked me to be his production manager instead.'

Disturbed to think this young man might resent her, Tansy was debating what to say when he spoke again.

'Khun Vin showed me photos of the samples you made for him, and I'm nowhere near your class. So working with you will teach me a lot.' The Rincome came in sight and he stopped at the entrance. 'Are you free to have dinner with me later?'

Unwilling to impose on him, she declined. 'I'm still a bit jet-lagged.'

'Another time, then. And by the way, it's OK for you to call me Deng!'

'Thanks. I'm Tansy.'

She stepped from the car and he jumped out and escorted her inside, then *wai*-ed her, fingers pointing upwards and palms together, head bent low to them. Anxious to be friendly, Tansy went to do the same, but he shook his head.

'No, no. You are my superior, and a superior shouldn't return a *wai*.'

'I'm sorry. I assumed it was the Thai version of a handshake—a sort of hello or goodbye.'

'It's more than that. It's a sign of respect, and the lower you bow your head when you make it, the more respectful it is.'

'Oh, dear, there are so many customs to remember I know I'll put my foot in it sooner or later!'

'Don't worry about it. We always make excuses for *farangs*!' he joked. 'Just make sure you don't *wai* to anyone who's of lower social status than yourself, and if you *do* decide to, never lower your head to them.'

'All this talk of social status wouldn't go down well in the West,' Tansy declared.

'That's because Westerners like to think all people are equal, whereas we believe people can be unequal yet have respect for each other.'

This wasn't a discussion she fancied getting into, and she changed the subject. 'Did you say you'd pick me up at eight-thirty in the morning?'

'Yes. I'll wait for you outside.'

Next morning, within moments of the agreed time, they were bowling towards San Kamphaeng, where Arunila had its two factories.

'We make all our silk on electric looms,' Deng informed her as they skirted tree-lined roads bordered by rice paddies and the dense green of orchards. 'But there's also a thriving cottage industry of hand-woven silk.'

'Is it different from ours?'

'Not in texture, but occasionally you'll find better designs.'

'Is it possible for me to see any?'

'No trouble. Most of the weaving is done in the back rooms of little shops that sell it by the metre.'

Arriving in the small town, they parked off the main street and headed for the silk shops. Here, in curtained-off sections in the back, two, three or four girls sat at old-fashioned wooden looms, their supple hands guiding strands of fibre, while their feet rocked a wooden bar backwards and forwards.

'The girls are so young!' Tansy exclaimed as they finally returned to the car. 'Either that, or I'm getting old!

'They *are* young,' Deng said wryly. 'They need strong eyes to work in such dim light.'

Tansy frowned, recollecting that none of the back-rooms had had windows, the only light filtering in through the fine lattice-work of the bamboo walls.

'How many metres can a girl produce a week?' she asked.

'About six. Impractical for us, if we're making a few thousand of each garment.'

'A pity. But maybe we can buy the copyright of some of the designs. I'll take a longer look when I have more time——'

She broke off as the Arunila factories came in sight, and for the next couple of hours went on a lightning tour. The silk factory was modern and couldn't be faulted, but the garment one was old-fashioned in lay-out and antiquated in machinery.

By the time she had visited every department she was ready to explode. Unless Mr Makram updated it, he had best forget about competing with the West.

'I'm doing my best to improve the quality and finish of our clothes,' Deng explained, noting her expression, 'but it takes time.'

Diplomatically silent, she followed him into the office he had prepared for her. It was large and bright, with a window giving a glimpse of the town half a mile away. But the desk was small, the chair hard, and there were no shelves or cupboards. Uncertain if he had arranged the furnishings, she hid her irritation. Thais were a proud people and disliked losing face.

'Any chance of a larger desk?' she enquired casually.

'No trouble. Do you want anything else?'

'A work table would be nice, and also two dress-maker's dummies. And if there's a chance of having some shelves... I like seeing materials around me when I'm sketching.'

'I'll get on to it immediately.'

Pleased by his eagerness to help her, she determined to get all her requests over with. 'Is there any hope of hiring two Western models? Thai girls are tiny, and buyers prefer seeing clothes modelled by the type of women they'll be selling to.'

Deng's flat, high-cheekboned face creased into a broad smile. 'I'm friendly with two Australian girls who are keen to stay here if they can find work. One *is* a model, and they both have great figures! I'll ask them to come and see you.'

'There you are,' a deep voice uttered, and Tansy swung round as Vin Makram sauntered in with the young woman she had seen with him in Bangkok. At close range she was even lovelier, her skin flawless, her eyes a clear light blue, and her hair so blonde it verged on silver.

'Miss Simmonds, I'd like you to meet Miss Ella Wainright. Her father owns Impo—they'll be importing and distributing our clothes in the States.'

'I've seen photos of the samples you made and I thought they were fabulous,' the girl said warmly. 'At least Arunila will now be producing *fashionable* clothes!'

'And well-finished ones, too!' Tansy assured her. 'By your next visit I think you'll notice a big improvement.'

'I'll be here for months yet.' Light blue eyes flicked to the man beside her, confirming Tansy's opinion as to where the girl's main interest lay.

'Do you work for your father?' she asked politely.

'I'm his roving trouble-shooter! That's why I'm here—to see Arunila delivers the goods! On time too. The summer collection has to be shown to the buyers by the second week in January.'

'I'm aware of that, Miss Wainright.'

From the corner of her eye, Tansy saw Vin Makram glance at his watch, as if eager to be gone. The American girl saw it too, for she slipped her arm possessively through his.

'I'll wait to hear from you, Miss Simmonds,' he stated, and, with what could only be described as a royal nod, went out, leaving Tansy with the distinct impression that he found the problems of Arunila more bother than they were worth. Not that she blamed him. The present profits were probably peanuts compared with his property empire. Still, he needn't have made his feelings quite so obvious.

Irrationally she found herself wondering what he was like away from business, and what kind of husband he would make. Did Thai men, like the Japanese, relegate their wives to the background? She couldn't see Ella Wainright standing for that. But why bother thinking of either of them? She had more important things to do.

'Will you book me on an early flight tomorrow and give me a list of our suppliers in Bangkok?' she asked Deng.

'No trouble. Is there anything I can do for you while you're away? Apart from altering this office?'

'Yes, there is. I want six of your best seamstresses to work solely on the samples we'll be showing the buyers.'

'That's easy. I'll clear out the room next door and install them there. Then you can keep an eagle eye on them—as long as you remember to treat them as if you're a dove!'

'Absolutely!' Tansy promised. 'Give orders with a smile, and if an employee makes a mess of something, pretend it's *my* fault!'

'You catch on quick!'

She was still amused by this when she entered her hotel room later in the day. Staring round it, she vowed that if her contract wasn't terminated she'd look for a furnished apartment. It would at least help her feel more at home.

An image of Vin Makram flashed before her, and she shook her head, regretting the unspoken antagonism between them. If she had been gifted with clairvoyance the day they had met in that dress shop, she would have bitten off her tongue before being so rude to him!

CHAPTER FOUR

EIGHT-THIRTY next morning found Tansy on her flight to Bangkok.

To her surprise, Deng had booked her into the Shangri-La overnight, and in the note he had penned her—together with the list of their suppliers—he enjoined her to 'have fun and relax'.

It was a kind gesture but she wished he had not made the decision for her. She had so much to do she could ill afford an extra day away. But she had been presented with a *fait accompli* and it was silly not to make the best of it.

She glanced at her holdall on the floor beside her. She always carried it round with her when working, for it enabled her to put in any accessory or sample of material that caught her eye. But she wasn't sure what had prompted her to put in a toothbrush and a change of underwear. Possibly the fear of the plane being delayed. Whatever, it meant she wouldn't look a total wreck when staying in such a luxurious hotel!

The day was as hectic as she had foreseen as she went from one trimmings firm to another. Though she spoke no Thai, and most of the people she met had a poor command of English—and in some cases none at all—she made it clear what she didn't like and why, and by the time she returned to her hotel in the evening she had found three suppliers willing to produce the quality goods she required.

Relaxing in a bath, she was sorry she had to eat alone. Pity Kevin wasn't here! She wondered where he was and what he was doing; somewhere exotic and something unusual that was for sure!

Twenty minutes later, Titian hair tumbling in a cascade of ringlets to her shoulders, stem-like waist encircled by a wide suede belt, and creamy skin emerging stamen-like from soft folds of cornflower-blue voile, she went down to the lower ground floor and the discreetly lit terrace where dinner was being served.

As she had expected, nearly all the tables were filled and, apart from the waiters, there wasn't a Thai among them! She was hesitating, uncertain whether to make for the coffee shop where she wouldn't feel conspicuous alone, when a waiter approached to lead her to a table.

Taking a deep breath, she followed him, aware of male eyes tracking her. Despite herself she was self-conscious, which was ridiculous, for she was an emancipated woman and didn't require a male to prop her ego.

Predictably, the table she was shown to was in a dark corner, and a spark of defiance—hell, she might be alone but she was entitled to the best available!—made her shake her head and point to another empty table in the centre of the terrace. The waiter palpably hesitated, then led her to it and handed her a menu.

Eyeing the prices, she nearly had a fit, then swiftly told herself not to be a fool. Deng had booked her in here and wouldn't expect her to eat from a street stall! Mind, she'd probably have a more authentic Thai meal if she did, but that sort of eating was best enjoyed as a twosome.

'Care for help with the menu, Miss Simmonds?' a cool male voice questioned.

Shock held Tansy rigid. Then she turned to the table on her right, where a tall, spare figure in a dark suit and black glasses was regarding her.

'Mr Makram! I—I didn't know you were in Bangkok.'

'I didn't know you were here either! When did you arrive?'

'This morning. I'm here on business,' she put in hurriedly, not wishing him to think she was taking time off.

'If you've no objection we can dine together,' he astonished her by saying.

The very notion promptly destroyed her appetite, but since to say so was unpardonable she smiled weakly, which he took as assent and joined her.

She didn't glance directly at him but was aware of his narrow-boned, bronze-skinned face with its straight, somewhat supercilious nose, and the enigmatic smile on the well-cut mouth. Wary of him though she was, she had to concede he was the handsomest man she had encountered. Yet was he really? He might have horrible foxy eyes!

'I can see my glasses bother you,' he broke into her thoughts. 'I don't wear them to be incognito.'

'I didn't think you did,' she murmured, imagining his annoyance if she said she assumed them to be an affectation! He already considered her rude, and she had no desire to compound it. 'It's disconcerting to talk to black lenses,' she admitted as he remained silent, 'though it makes you look awfully mysterious!'

White teeth gleamed as he smiled. 'The only mystery is when the specialist will allow me to discard them.'

Tansy coloured, disconcerted. 'I didn't realise there was anything wrong with——'

'Nothing serious,' he broke in. 'I was stung in the eye a few months ago, and have to keep all light from it until it heals. For a while I wore an eye-patch, but found it more bother than glasses.'

'You must have resembled a pirate,' she blurted out, instantly regretting it as a black eyebrow rose.

'You mean Long John Silver?'

'You know *Treasure Island*?' she said in surprise.

'I had an English and American education. It's an advantage to be cosmopolitan.'

Sensing a reprimand, she hurriedly bent to the menu.

'May I choose you a typically Thai meal?' he suggested.

'As long as it isn't typically hot!'

'I promise you it won't be.'

Stretching out his arm without raising it, and keeping his hand palm down, he beckoned their waiter and placed his order. As the man moved off, Tansy couldn't help commenting on the unusual way he had been summoned.

'It's considered rude to point to anyone,' Vin Makram explained.

'Thank goodness you told me, or I'd have been rude in every restaurant!'

'I'm afraid we've a long list of "dos and don'ts", but luckily *farangs*—foreigners—aren't expected to know them all. The one you *should* remember, though, is that Thais regard the head as the most sacred part of your body, and the feet as the most lowly. So never sit with your foot pointing at anyone.'

'I know you have to take off your shoes before entering a private home or a temple,' she murmured, 'but I'd no idea about pointing.'

'Not touching someone's head is equally important,' her host added. 'You may touch a baby's head, and of course lovers do as they wish in private.'

A *frisson* shivered through her as he said the word 'lovers'. But it was only because it was strange to hear so aloof a man use such an emotive term. Yet aloofness didn't negate passion, though it could well negate tenderness. Annoyed to be thinking of him in this manner, she rushed into conversation.

'I didn't know I was booked into this hotel until I saw the voucher attached to my ticket. In fact I was set to fly back tonight.'

'Don't you like the Shangri-La?'

'It's wonderful. But I meant the cost of staying over.'

A smile miraculously softened the man's haughty expression. Drat those glasses of his! She'd have a far better feel of his character if she saw his eyes. How right the poets were to call them the windows of the soul. When they were closed or hidden, a person was an enigma.

'Don't worry over the expense, Miss Simmonds. A few nights here won't bankrupt the company.'

'I'm aware of that, but I didn't want you thinking I'm extravagant.'

'It wasn't the first thought that entered my head when I saw you tonight!' Light caught his spectacles as he surveyed her. 'I was struck by how beautifully you model your own clothes. You *did* design the dress you're wearing?'

Cheeks red as peonies, she nodded, not bothering to explain that it was in her wardrobe because she hadn't managed to sell it. Such information was definitely not for Mr Makram's well-shaped ears!

'Now you've cleared your conscience because you're staying here,' he said into the silence, 'I suggest we enjoy our dinner.'

The meal he ordered was a sample of many dishes, and she was gratified by the trouble he had taken to give her such a wide example of the cuisine of his country. By the time dinner was over their talk had ranged over many topics, and she was amazed by the similarity of their tastes.

'Fancy a stroll?' he enquired as they left the terrace.

Taking her silence for consent, he took her arm to guide her, and her body tingled at his touch. It had nothing to do with him as a man, she assured herself. It was simply that his aura of command made her feel she should curtsy!

Pushing aside the fanciful notion, she stared round her. They were walking through the gardens, the branches of the low trees strung with sparkling silver lights, giving the feeling of fairyland. On her left lay the white bulk of the hotel, and ahead the large, free-form pool, desolate without its fringe of sunbeds and blue umbrellas.

They strolled twice round it, neither of them speaking. Tansy was amazed to be at ease with this man, and wondered if his being foreign lessened her self-consciousness. Her mouth curved wryly. How insular she was. If anyone was foreign, it was she!

Was that how Mr Makram saw her? And did he think the same of Ella Wainright, whose blondeness was so at variance with his brooding darkness? Did

her possessiveness include marriage? Though Mr
Makram was gorgeous as a dark Greek god, his cultural and religious roots were totally different from
Western ones. Yet it was said love could bridge any
gap, and the charisma emanating from him was tangible enough to span the widest chasm!

He paused by the far side of the pool, leaning on
the wooden rail to stare out across the wide river which
ran like a main artery through the city. Upstream, a
graceful bridge spanned the water, tiny cars—like
diamond-studded ants—racing briskly along it. It
could have been New York or London, Tansy mused,
were it not for the spires of the temples which dotted
the city like daisies a meadow.

'This is such a beautiful country,' she murmured.

'So is England. Do you live in London?'

'Yes, but I was born in Bristol. I left it to go to
design college.'

'I bet you were a banner-waving student!'

'You only say that because of my hair!'

He chuckled. 'And your manner. You have strong
opinions and no hesitation in expressing them.'

'Yes, well...' He had given her an opportunity and
she felt obliged to take it. 'I'm sorry I was rude when
we met in your shop. I'm not sorry for what I said,
only for not being more diplomatic.'

'A rather two-edged apology, but I'll accept it!'

She waited for him to make his own, recollecting
how high-handedly he had snubbed her, but he simply
continued his questioning of her.

'What did you do when you left college?'

'Struggled! Only in the beginning,' she rushed on.
'Once I was established I was busy night and day.'

Well, that was true—busy making clothes and not selling them!

'Mrs Gray said you were one of her brightest students,' he commented. 'Did you have many offers like mine?'

Tansy hesitated, sorry she had not been more honest with him. But it was too late now. 'I preferred being a free agent,' she parried.

'Why did you accept *my* offer?'

'It was a challenge.'

'Which redheads enjoy.'

'It isn't red, it's auburn,' she said automatically.

'Sorry. These glasses make it hard for me to discriminate shades of colour.'

He put his hand to the frame and she instantly reached out and caught his arm, then stepped back in confusion. 'Sorry. I-I was afraid you were going to take them off.'

'Don't apologise for your concern.' He dropped his arm to his side. 'Even through my glasses I can tell your hair is your crowning glory.'

'The bane of my life,' she corrected. 'As a child I went through torture combing it, and at school I was called "beetroot"!'

His laugh rang out. 'I can imagine your reaction!'

'A very combative one,' she confessed. 'If I have any children I hope they have straight black hair!' She stopped abruptly, horrified in case he imagined she was harbouring dreams about *him*. 'At least if your hair's straight,' she babbled on, 'you can wear it any——'

'Why are you embarrassed?' he cut in.

'I'm not.'

'You are, and it isn't necessary. Your comment was perfectly understandable.' He glanced at his watch. 'Much as I'm enjoying our conversation, I'll have to call it a day. I've a seven a.m. breakfast meeting.'

'You should have told me earlier.'

'And given you an excuse to rush off?'

Unnerved, she started walking towards the hotel.

'After my meeting,' he said, keeping pace with her, 'I'd like to show you around Bangkok.'

'I'm going back in the morning.'

'Catch a later plane. I'll meet you in the lobby at nine-thirty.'

'But——'

'Don't argue with your employer!'

'Are you asking me out as an employer?'

Her bluntness startled him and she was pleased. But not for long was this man at a disadvantage, and his reply was swift and smooth.

'It's good public relations to be on friendly terms with one's key personnel, Miss Simmonds. And when it comes to the success of Arunila, you are the most important key.'

There was only one answer to make to this, and she did.

'I'll see you at nine-thirty then, Mr Makram. Goodnight.'

CHAPTER FIVE

NEXT morning, going to meet Mr Makram—it was alien to think of him as Khun Vin and oddly disturbing to think of him as Vin—Tansy was sorry she hadn't gone out earlier and bought another dress, instead of making do with the one she had worn yesterday.

There was no sign of him in the lobby, which thronged with chattering groups, some arriving, others departing, and many waiting to be taken on tours.

Although she was doing her best to be nonchalant about her forthcoming day, the instant she saw him— tall and elegant in charcoal-grey trousers and paler silk sweater—her thumping heart told her she had been fooling herself. She was thrilled to be spending the day with him; excited by his presence and intrigued by his astute brain and occasionally acerbic tongue— as long as the acerbity wasn't directed at *her*!

Many female eyes watched him walk towards her, and she knew it wasn't only his wide-shouldered figure that attracted attention, nor the enveloping black spectacles, so much as his haughty disregard at being the cynosure of all eyes.

'Good morning, Mr Makram,' she said coolly.

'Good morning. You're not merely on time, you're early!'

'It's bad tactics to keep one's boss waiting.'

'Not your boss today please, and not Mr Makram either, or I'll have to "Miss Simmonds" you all day!'

Pulses racing, she managed a cool smile, hoping that when it came to it she'd also be able to manage his first name. She edged towards the street but he steered her down the wide, curving stairs to the terrace, and from there to the wooden landing-stage by the river's edge, where hotel guests were waiting for the boats that plied between the three luxury hotels fronting this stretch of water.

Instead of joining the queue, they boarded a small, newly painted motor launch. It rocked beneath Tansy's feet and she clutched at Mr Makram's arm. No, at Vin's arm. Lord, she'd never get used to calling him that.

Letting go of him, she went towards a cushion-covered seat. As she did, the launch shot across the water and she slithered helplessly over the deck to the shiny silver rail. Before she hit it, Vin Makram leapt in front of it, his body taking the full impact of hers.

For a brief moment they were locked together, her face pressed into the warmth of his neck. His skin was soft as silk against her mouth, the scent of it like jasmine in her nostrils. She was frighteningly aware of the strength of the arms encompassing her, the solid wall of his chest upon the softness of her breasts, and his hipbone hard against her thigh.

He was the first to recover and, stepping away from her, he guided her to a seat. 'Sorry about that. Our "captain" has more enthusiasm than judgement!'

'It was my fault for not holding on.'

'You won't need to in future. If he goes more than one knot an hour, I'll scalp him!'

He sat opposite her, his black hair ruffling in the breeze that even their decorous speed raised. Once more she imagined him as a pirate, and warned herself that behind his charming manner he was a ruthless man, and definitely not one to cross.

It reminded her that if he disliked her designs he had the right to send her back to England—and definitely would! If only she hadn't agreed to that clause. Despondency swamped her, and with an effort she shook it off. What the hell! If he sent her packing she'd get a year's severance pay. Enough to open her own workshop again. Yet she wasn't going to fail, and it was negative to think otherwise.

She gazed at the scene around her. The olive-green water was murky with mud and the blue sky was washed pale by the sun. On her left, a long line of slow-moving river barges—linked by ropes and laden with timber—was steaming upstream, while on her right was a water bus filled with schoolchildren in regulation navy and white, waving to her.

But it was the black-haired, golden-skinned man touching distance away from her of whom she was most conscious, for he had the strange power to make her weak at the knees!

'Where are we heading?' she asked huskily.

'The Grand Palace.' As he spoke, their launch turned into a narrow waterway. 'If you look on your right you'll see the newer part of the city, and this *klong* we're on—you'd call it a canal,' he added, 'has turned the land on our left into an island.'

'What's on it?'

'Government offices, the palace, and the temple of the Emerald Buddha.'

The launch glided to a stop at a landing-stage, and they stepped out and walked along a tree-lined road towards the shining white walls that enclosed the precinct round the temples and the pink-coloured palace, with its intricately carved stepped roofs of red and green tiles.

'It's like something out of *The King and I*!' Tansy exclaimed, and he chuckled.

'I guess that's how most Westerners still think of us, but in the last eight years we've become a country of the future.'

'That applies to almost the entire Far East,' she agreed. 'It's becoming as industrialised as the West. Rather a shame, I think.'

'Not if we manage to retain the beauty of the past. And Thailand can hold on to it more easily than other countries.'

'Why is that?'

'Because its past is closely linked to its Buddhist religion, and religion is a daily part of Thai life.'

Tansy tried—and failed—to imagine Vin Makram prostrating himself on the floor in a temple. Somehow he seemed too proud. She bit back a sigh, and wondered whether she would ever feel entirely at home with him or his country.

'Come,' he said. 'We have much to see.'

On close inspection, the Grand Palace was aptly named. Its royal residence had been designed by an English architect but was predominantly Italian Renaissance in style, though the King for whom it had been built had insisted on having traditional Thai stepped roofs, each one tiled in green and red and edged with gold.

Only the main reception-rooms were open to the public, and the one which impressed Tansy most was the Throne Room. Here, under a nine-tiered white umbrella, the King received foreign ambassadors and other important visitors.

'Have you met the King?' she asked.

'Frequently. Our friendship with the Royal Family goes back years.'

This information, casually offered, put Vin even further out of her orbit; not that she had ever been in it, she reminded herself. He was a star in a galaxy of his own!

Irritated by her fanciful notions, she concentrated on sightseeing, and followed him to a graceful white building where a large, timber-lined chamber housed a black throne inlaid with mother-of-pearl.

'All the wood here came from the forests around Chiang Mai,' Vin apprised her. 'The tree trunks were dragged to the nearest river by elephants, and were then roped on to rafts and sent here by water.'

'Are the waterways still used for transport?'

'I'm afraid trucks have taken over, but elephants are used for carrying timber from the forests.' As he spoke, he guided her to the State Hall, where another throne, boat-shaped this time, dominated the room. 'In the olden days this was hidden by golden curtains,' he explained, 'and you weren't allowed to see it unless the King was sitting on it.'

'Why?'

'Tradition.'

'I should have guessed!'

White teeth gleamed as he ushered her into the courtyard, and she paused to admire an intricately carved door. 'Does this lead anywhere special?'

'To a garden, and what used to be the royal harem.'

'Have *you* ever fancied a harem?' she asked mischievously.

'Only in my dreams. In reality, one wife is problem enough!'

'You sound as if you've been married!'

'Not yet. But I think all intimate relationships can be tricky, and those between men and women particularly so. They have such contrasting attitudes that it makes marriage like an obstacle race.'

Tansy wished she had the nerve to carry on this conversation, but discretion won the day.

For the next hour they wandered the grounds, past saffron-robed monks, their heads shaved, their faces serene, and throngs of visitors and guides—a few speaking English, the majority Japanese and German.

'What say we rest a while?' Vin Makram suggested as she dabbed her forehead with a tissue.

'I'm fine,' Tansy said quickly. 'Can't we see a bit more? Something close by?' she pressed.

'Wat Phra Keo.'

'What?'

'Not what.' Again white teeth flashed in a smile as he spelled it out. 'WAT. The word means temple, and the Emerald Buddha is kept in the one I just mentioned. It's the holiest relic in Thailand.'

'Then lead on, Macduff,' she misquoted. 'I've got second wind!'

Crossing the crowded compound, they reached the golden-spired temple adjoining the Grand Palace, and walking through the Assembly Hall, where large urns held the ashes of dead royals, they reached a stairway flanked by bronze lions.

Here, her escort removed his shoes, and Tansy did the same, glad she had pretty feet and no corns! Predictably, Vin wore silk socks, and she smiled, then hastily smothered it. But unfortunately not before he had seen it.

'May I share the joke?'

'It's your socks. Are you always so impeccably turned out?'

'Only when I don't have sandals! I find shoes without socks uncomfortable.' His head lowered. 'I see *you* don't.' He paused. 'Your feet are perfect.'

Flushing, Tansy wriggled her toes, marvelling anew how easily this man made her feel gauche. It seemed she should not only guard her tongue but her smiles too!

Cheeks still burning, she mounted the steps to the inner temple, skirting golden pillars decorated with a mosaic of colourful tiles, to enter the main chapel.

Expecting quietness, she was surprised by the bustle. 'Is it always as noisy?'

'Often it's noisier! We don't regard religion as something solemn to be observed only one day a week. To us, it's an everyday part of our lives.'

How true, Tansy reflected, noticing several families sitting on the floor chatting, while others prostrated themselves, and still more wandered the side aisles. For a while she watched in silence, then curiosity got the better of her.

'Why isn't anyone using the centre aisle?' she asked.

'It's reserved for the King.'

'Tradition?'

'Clever of you to guess!'

Catching her hand, he pulled her up a short flight of steps into the small, most sacred chapel of all. Blue-tiled and serene, in its centre a gilded altar rose some thirty feet high, and atop it, beneath the shade of a nine-tiered umbrella, sat the Emerald Buddha. It was carved from a single piece of green jade, and its body was covered by an enamel-coated solid gold robe.

'I'm sorry it's in its winter dress,' the man beside her said. 'It wears less in summer, though you get the best view of it in the rainy season. That's one of the King's duties—changing the Buddha's garments.'

'If I'm still here when the rains come, I'll make a point of seeing it. It's exquisite.'

'Why shouldn't you be here?' came the abrupt question.

'You may have sent me back to England by then!'

'You don't genuinely believe that. You have too much confidence in yourself.'

'It isn't *my* confidence that's in question,' she retorted, 'it's *yours* in me. And the "right of dismissal" which you put in our contract shows you still have doubts about my ability.'

'I hadn't met you then,' he said quietly. 'Now that I have, I'm certain you will prove me wrong.'

Trust him to have the last word! Tossing her head, she descended the steps and, searching for a less emotive subject as they strolled in the direction of the river, said, 'How old is the Emerald Buddha?'

'No one knows. It was found near Chiang Mai in 1436, but it's far older and comes from either Ceylon or Cambodia. Originally it was covered in plaster and painted with gold leaf, and it wasn't until it was being sent to the king of Chiang Mai and the plaster broke that they discovered it was made of jade.'

'How exciting when something like that happens.' They reached the launch and climbed aboard. 'I mean to find a treasure and then discover it's even more fabulous than you imagined!'

'I hope that will apply to my discovery of *you*,' he answered smoothly.

Tansy was still digesting this remark when he spoke again.

'After lunch, I thought I'd give you a tour of the city.'

'Lovely. But I'm happy to skip lunch. The heat takes away my appetite.'

'It will, until you're used to it. Meanwhile, cut out stodge and concentrate on protein.'

'By stodge, you mean rice?'

'Good heavens, no!'

He was so horrified that she giggled. Rice was a staple part of Thai diet, and they'd as soon do without it as a Brit his tea or an American his coffee!

'I was thinking of cakes and sweets,' he asserted. 'Though you don't look as if you indulge.'

Despite his eyes being masked, she knew they were ranging over her, and was annoyingly aware of her body's response to it: her stomach muscles tightening, her nipples hardening.

'You're quite wrong!' she said quickly. 'When I'm busy I live on chocolate!'

Anxious to stop further comment on her figure, she pretended absorption in her surroundings, and he did not speak until they were walking through the hotel gardens to the lobby.

'Even if you don't want to eat,' he stated, 'you might like to rest before going out again.'

'I'm fine, if you are,' she replied, 'though I wish I could change into a fresh dress. I didn't come equipped for an overnight stay.'

'I'd never guess it from your appearance.'

'How gallant of you! But I'm hot and crumpled and I know it shows!'

'I promise you it doesn't. But if it worries you, it's easy to remedy. There's an Arunila boutique close by.'

'That desperate I'm not!'

His smile was thin-edged, and without comment he grasped her elbow and propelled her out of the hotel and down the steep incline to the street. It was lined with little stores, many open-fronted, and he headed towards one displaying batik dresses.

Approving the subtle colours and simple styles, Tansy chose a pale green shift, and as she went to open her purse he restrained her and handed the assistant a five-hundred-*baht* note. Recalling his terse comment last night about expenses, she knew better than to protest at his spending the equivalent of ten pounds on her.

'Aren't you going to try it on?' he enquired.

'It isn't necessary. It's loose-fitting and I'll shape it with a belt.'

'I can see you aren't the average Arunila customer!'

'You can say that again! Which reminds me, how come you were in the shop that day?'

'I was curious to find out why our clothes weren't selling.'

'I certainly told you!'

'And how!'

They entered the lobby and she paused. 'Give me ten minutes to change, and I'll meet you here.'

'Take longer. I'm not impatient.'

'I can't believe that.'

'Today is a vacation for me,' he vouchsafed, 'and I enjoy relaxing and taking things as they come.' As if to prove it, he sauntered over to an armchair. 'Don't rush, Tansy. I'm happy to wait for you.'

CHAPTER SIX

DESPITE knowing Vin Makram didn't mind waiting for her, Tansy returned to the lobby with one minute to spare from the ten she had promised.

Although the batik shift was simple, the colour gave lustre to her skin, and the scoop neck disclosed the gentle curve of her breasts. It had a long sash of its own material and she had cut in in two, using one part to tie round her waist, and the other to twine in the plait into which she had pulled back her hair. It wasn't a style she normally adopted, for she considered it made her appear too young, but the heat of the day had impelled her to lift it off her face and neck.

The sharp turn of Vin's head as she walked beside him indicated his awareness of it, though it wasn't until they were walking down the street that he remarked on it.

'With that ribboned plait of yours I'd take you for eighteen,' he declared.

'Knowing what's ahead of me at Arunila I feel eighty!'

He stopped walking so abruptly that she bumped into him, and drew back with an embarrassed apology.

'What's worrying you?' he demanded.

For an instant she hesitated, then decided to be frank. He might be her boss but she refused to regard him as an ogre out to destroy her. 'I'll do everything in my power to design a collection that's right for your market, but style is a matter of taste and I think you may be over-critical. Even if you dislike my designs, you should allow the buyers to decide.'

There was a long silence, broken only by the strident sound of a passing motorbike.

'You're forgetting one thing,' he said slowly. 'Of all the samples shown to me, I chose yours. I didn't do it from my knowledge of fashion but from a gut instinct that *your* talent is outstanding.'

Pink-cheeked, Tansy forced herself to stare into the black lenses. She couldn't see his eyes but she felt she owed it to him to let him see hers.

'Then it seems as if, for the second time in our acquaintance, I owe you an apology, K-Khun—Khun Vin.'

'Apology accepted—and may I remind you to drop the *Khun*? Plain Vin will do fine.'

'Hardly plain!' she rejoined without thinking. 'I'd say commanding or imperious.'

He chuckled. 'That's more like it. I was just thinking you've been polite too long!'

Hastily she turned her head. 'What's on the agenda for this afternoon?'

'No more sightseeing! Simply a gentle amble round Bangkok to give you the feel of it.'

A taxi drew alongside them but he shook his head and hailed a passing *tuk-tuk* which, at close quarters, resembled a two-seater dodgem car perched on a three-wheeled motor-cycle.

Tansy clambered in and he followed. There was ample room for two—indeed she had seen three adults sitting in one—but it brought her uncomfortably close to him, and closer still when the *tuk-tuk* turned a corner sharply and she slid along the narrow seat into his hard thigh. Automatically he steadied her, and she moved back into her corner and gripped the side to make sure she didn't slide again.

Because it was small, the *tuk-tuk* had the nerve-racking ability to squeeze through spaces that, to Tansy's appalled eyes, were far too narrow for safety! And then the noise of it! The rough, two-stroke engine made a jet seem quiet, and its breakneck speed had her closing her eyes as they zigzagged between buses, cars and coaches.

'Don't be scared,' Vin placated when she yelped as they missed a bus with millimetres to spare. 'There are thousands of *tuk-tuks* here and they hardly have any accidents.'

'I'm trying to believe you!' she said through gritted teeth.

'Shall we stop and take a cab?'

'No. I can see you're determined to show me the real Thailand and I'm equally determined to enjoy it—even if it kills me!'

Grinning, he leaned forward and spoke to the driver, who nodded and slowed down. But her relief was short-lived, for within seconds they were going faster than ever.

'Trying to get them to go slow,' Vin apologised, 'is harder than harnessing a gazelle!'

Ahead of them traffic lights turned red, and they stopped. The cool breeze that had been blowing against Tansy ceased, and she was acutely aware of the heat of the city, the petrol fumes, the burning pavements. Sweat erupted on her skin and she fanned herself with her purse.

'We'll be better off walking,' Vin murmured, and, paying off the driver, helped her out.

They were in a part of Bangkok she hadn't visited before. The streets were wide and teemed with traffic, the pavements so closely lined with stalls competing for business with the stores that it was impossible to cross the road until you found a gap between one stall and another.

The goods on offer were amazing: clothes for all sizes, in all colours, in all styles, from copies of designer chic to punk grot. There were bags by the hundred, belts by the thousand, shorts and shirts by the million, most of them copies of brand goods, and so similar to the originals that it was hard to spot they weren't.

It wasn't easy walking, for the pavements were a sea of bodies moving like a sluggish tide. Yet everyone was good-tempered despite the heat and noise. Tourists were busy bartering and happily walking off with 'bargains', while stall holders equally happily pocketed ten times what the goods cost them.

'Vendors have two different prices,' Vin said in her ear. 'One for visitors and one for Thais.'

'I bet they charge us double!'

'Quadruple, more likely! But it's still less than you'd pay in your own country.'

Abruptly he pulled her left, into a world of alleys lined with more stalls and tiny shops. All of them sold wearing apparel, with the emphasis on clothes. Despite the narrowness of the alleys, motorbikes frequently drove along them, slowly but noisily, and browsing shoppers were jostled by young boys wheeling sharp-pointed trolleys stacked high with bulging plastic bags full of garments.

'Do you have markets like this in England?' Vin enquired as they emerged into one of the back streets and were able to glimpse the blue sky above them.

'None as big as this. Did you bring me here for any special reason?'

'No. I assumed you'd enjoy it.'

Her soft mouth curved upwards. 'That's what's known as a busman's holiday.'

Disconcerted, he frowned. 'So it is. I hope you'll forgive me?'

She nodded, but it brought home to her that his offer to take her sightseeing had been prompted by their business relationship and not a desire for her company. Yet why should she have thought otherwise? If she hadn't signed up with Arunila, their paths wouldn't have crossed again. Without her knowing why, despondency washed over her, and despite the bustle and teeming crowds she felt desperately alone.

'You've suddenly gone quiet,' the man at her side said.

'I'm sorry. I—I was thinking of home.' Tears gushed into her eyes and she fumbled in her purse for a tissue. A pristine handkerchief was pushed into her hand and gratefully she dabbed away the tears. 'Silly of me to carry on like this—once I start work proper I'll be fine.'

'Then I'll make it my business to keep your nose to the grindstone!'

His humour helped banish her blues and she squared her shoulders. 'I'm better now, thank you.'

'Good.' He reached for his handkerchief but she held on to it.

'I'll wash it before I give it back to you. I've put mascara on it.'

'Beats me why you wear any.' His head lowered towards her, his hair black satin in the sunlight. 'You have the longest lashes I've ever seen. I'd never have guessed they were false.'

'They aren't!' Indignation died as he laughed. 'It's mean to tease me while your face is half hidden. It gives you an unfair advantage.'

'A man must use every advantage he can when dealing with a woman! But don't rush to re-examine your contract. When it comes to business, I'm fair and square!'

'So Diana Gray told me.'

He raised perfectly arched eyebrows—the first occasion she had seen them both, for his aviator-type spectacles normally hid them. 'Thanks! Such a generous compliment deserves a gift.'

This proved to be a small plastic bag containing two slices of freshly cut pineapple, which he bought from a fruit stall they were passing. He bought a bag for himself too, and without embarrassment took a hearty bite.

Tansy followed suit, hastily wiping her chin as the juice ran. 'It's delicious! Much tastier than any I've had in England.'

'That's because they aren't picked green and left to ripen on the boat. The same applies to our bananas.'

'My favourite fruit. If they made it into perfume, I'd be first in line for a bottle!'

'I like the one you're wearing. What is it?'

'I'm not wearing any.'

'So the lovely smell is you?'

Heat coursed through her body and, pretending she hadn't heard him, she bit into another slice of pineapple and quickened her step.

For the next few hours they wandered the city, with Vin occasionally regaling her with items of interest, yet knowing when to let her absorb the sights and sounds for herself. She had known Bangkok was large, but hadn't realised it was forty times the size of Chiang Mai.

Without doubt it was a boom city, with a bewildering mix of the ancient and modern: the serenity of the East and the go-ahead style of the West. At one moment she was in the hushed precincts of a temple, and the next picking her way past a building site. Indeed office blocks, hotels and large department stores were springing up everywhere.

'If building continues at this rate, Bangkok will be ruined!' Vin exclaimed as they turned into Sukhumvit Road, one of the smart shopping thoroughfares.

Tansy appreciated his criticism, but personally enjoyed the juxtaposition of old and new. A modern shopping mall sprouted next to an old market; a shining black Mercedes purred past a noisy *tuk-tuk*; a crowd of miniskirted teenagers politely gave way to a barefoot, saffron-robed monk no older than they were; a tiny Chinese pagoda perched atop a dingy tailor's shop; a wrinkled crone crouched on the pavement clipping orchid blossoms into garlands, while behind her was a window filled with the latest health foods.

It was only as Tansy paused at an intersection and glanced at her watch that she saw it was nearly five.

'Heck! My plane goes at seven and I'll miss it.'

'No, you won't.' A muscled bronze arm hailed a passing cab.

'Are you returning on the same flight?' she asked as they scrambled in.

'Regrettably not. I've a conference in Phuket—it's an island off the south coast—and I'll be there about ten days.'

Knowing she wouldn't be seeing him till then was so disturbing that she hastily sought for a reason. Of course! She'd only miss him because he was her one link with England. A tenuous link maybe, considering the only person they had in common was Diana Gray, but a link none the less.

'Don't forget me while I'm away,' he said unexpectedly.

'How can I? You're like Big Brother watching me— *1984* and all that!'

'Am I so frightening?'

'Not today,' she confessed. 'But you *can* be somewhat aloof.'

'Frequently it's a man's way of resisting a beautiful woman.'

Did this mean he was no longer resisting her? And did he really find her beautiful? Hastily she pushed the questions aside.

'Trouble is,' Vin went on, 'when a man decides not to resist any longer, he is often not forgiven for his earlier behaviour.'

Convinced he was flirting with her, Tansy was at a loss how to act. In normal circumstances it would have presented no problem, but in view of their working relationship, to say nothing of the difference in their social position, she had to tread a very circumspect path. Besides, he was a damnably attractive man and she could easily fall for him.

'No comment, Tansy?'

'No comment.'

'One day I won't allow you to play safe.'

One day... It was a strange remark and she was still puzzling over it as they entered the hotel and Vin paused by the porter's desk to order a cab to take her to the airport.

'Thank you for a wonderful day,' she said as he escorted her to a lift.

'I'm glad you enjoyed it.' His hand came out to touch the wide black frames that blocked all side light from his eyes. 'I hope you'll have some designs to show me when I return to Chiang Mai.'

Stifling the impulse to tell him the only design in her head right now was on him, she said aloud, 'Don't expect too much—I have to find a theme first.'

'And if you can't?'

'I refuse to consider such a question!'

'Good. I admire a woman with confidence.'

As long as it didn't make her argumentative! Tansy reflected as she stepped into the lift.

Her last glimpse of Vin was of his dark head silhouetted by the gilded wall behind him: a handsome, charismatic man of strong opinions and determination. A man of the East who, for all his modernity, was unlikely to find his ideal woman in the West.

And don't you forget it, Tansy Simmonds, she warned herself, or you'll be asking for trouble.

CHAPTER SEVEN

WHETHER it was a desire to please Vin Makram or the natural workings of creativity, Tansy didn't know, but when she awoke at dawn next morning in her bedroom at the Rincome Hotel she had the theme she had been searching for.

As always when taken by the Muse, her energy was demonic, and for two weeks she worked far into the nights, taking meals at her desk and leaving it only to return to the hotel to sleep.

When the bulk of her sketches was completed she showed them to Deng, and was gratified by his vociferous approval.

'I'd have liked to use embroidery on some of the clothes,' she admitted, 'but I wasn't sure I'd be able to get it done here.'

'Let me show you something,' Deng said, and hurried out, returning with a large leatherbound book—old and clearly valuable—of photographs of traditional Thai dress. 'We can easily get this type of embroidery made,' he explained, 'but not in time for January.'

'May I borrow the book anyway? It's fascinating.'

'Please accept it as a gift.'

She was reluctant to take such an expensive present, but knowing Thais were generous as well as friendly she was worried that if she refused it, Deng would regard it as a rebuff.

'It's awfully kind of you,' she murmured. 'I'll treasure it.

Expecting Vin to return in two weeks, Tansy was disappointed when the third week came and went without news of him, and she was hard put to it not to call his secretary to find out when he was due back, prevented only by the fear of his misinterpreting her desire to see him. But time was running out, and the longer she had to wait approval of her sketches, the shorter time they would have to make the samples.

Irritated and on edge, she spent the weekend re-sketching some of her designs—quite unnecessarily, she knew, but it kept her occupied—and Monday morning she dressed with great care, her tried and trusted means of keeping up her spirits, and set off for the factory.

Against the periwinkle-blue of her softly tailored linen suit, her hair glowed like burgundy wine. In Bangkok the humidity had made it curly, but in the crisper air of the north it fell into soft waves, give or take a few tendrils which curled round her face. She had lost weight these past two weeks and it was ap-parent in the hollows beneath her cheekbones. But she liked the deceptively fragile air it gave her, and heightened it by using no blusher.

'Khun Vin's back!' Deng greeted her as she entered her office.

Feeling as if she had drunk a glass of champagne too quickly, she hurriedly sat at her drawing-board. 'Have you spoken to him, then?'

'No, his secretary called me.'

Tansy nodded. Arunila was a small cog in the large wheel of the Makram empire and it was unlikely Vin could visit her today. Yet telling herself this and believing it were two different stories, and when noon came with not even a call from him, she was inordinately disappointed.

In an effort to forget him she toured the factory, Deng beside her, and occasionally paused to chat to one or other of the women, using him as an interpreter.

'The friendly atmosphere is very noticeable here,' she commented when they were back in her office. 'Is it like this in all factories?'

'In good ones, yes. If you want a successful business you have to keep your employees happy by throwing parties for them.'

'It's the same in England. Most firms do it at Christmas, and some also arrange a day out in summer.'

Deng's broad-cheeked face creased into a grin. 'Thais expect more than that! A little party at least every month. Nothing fancy, of course, just a chance for everybody to have a good time.'

Tansy went to reply, the words dying on her lips at the entry of a dark-suited man, his bronze skin a deeper tan than she had remembered, a third of his face still hidden by dark spectacles.

'Good morning, Khun Vin.' Tansy deliberately made her greeting formal, and the faint lift of his mouth showed his awareness of it.

'Hello, Tansy,' he responded. 'Any designs to show me?'

'Sixty,' she replied, lifting out a sheaf of papers from a drawer and setting them on top of her desk.

He strode over to them, stopping partly behind her to study them. His breath was warm on the side of her neck and she trembled but remained where she was, afraid he might notice if she drew back. What was the matter with her, reacting to him like a nervous schoolgirl? Yet there was nothing girlish in her physical awareness of him, nor her body's response to his nearness.

Resolutely she concentrated on the sketches, but here too lay danger, for she was painfully aware of his lean, strong-fingered hands taking hold of them one by one. For what seemed an eternity he continued appraising them, and Tansy forced herself to keep her expression blank.

'Excellent,' he stated finally, moving away from her. 'As soon as the samples are ready I'll call in our advertising agency and have them prepare a campaign for our shops.'

Tansy frowned. 'When women pay our sort of prices they like to know the clothes have been created by a *person*, not a shop. I'm not saying this because I'm the designer, but because it will help sales if we give Arunila a human aspect.'

The mobile mouth, close to hers, albeit several inches above, thinned. 'Surely that only applies to women who go to top couturiers? Our customers will come to us because they'll be getting first class styling at affordable prices. So it's the name of the *shop* that counts.'

'In part, yes. But publicising a person makes for greater interest. I feel very strongly about it.'

There was silence, and from the corner of her eye she saw Deng standing stiff as a ramrod, as if awaiting an explosion. But Vin was relaxed, one hand at his side, the other in the pocket of his jacket.

'I take your point,' he drawled. 'Neither of us is wrong, but in this instance you are more right than I am!'

The apology was typical of him, and she bit back a smile.

'Publicising you will certainly be easier,' he went on. 'You'll make a striking model for your clothes.'

'I wasn't expecting to pose in them,' she said hastily. 'We should have experienced models for that.'

'Then how can we publicise you?'

'In articles and radio and TV interviews. It will cost money, but——'

'It will be worth it.' He nodded towards the sketches. 'These are marvellous.'

Gratified, she none the less felt a warning was called for. 'I only hope the samples are exact copies of my designs. But it won't be easy with the seamstresses we have.'

'Then hire others.' Vin swung round on Deng. 'Is there any difficulty doing so?'

Deng lowered his head in respect, for in Thai society status was all. 'There aren't enough skilled women here and we have to retrain those we have.'

'I understood you were engaging some from Bangkok?'

Deng nodded, as if in confirmation, and Tansy, who knew he was doing nothing of the sort, hid her astonishment. But the moment Deng left the office, Vin grimaced cynically.

'I'm well aware Deng hasn't tried to hire new staff, but if I'd confronted him with it he'd have lost face. Like this, he'll do as I want without my giving him an order.'

'Can't one *ever* give orders?' she asked in dismay.

'Certainly. But gently, and with a smile.'

'You aren't gentle and smiling with *me*!'

There was a noticeable pause, then a hand raked back thick black hair. 'I treat you as a Westerner and my equal. But between Thais there are rigid rules of conduct, and if I wish to show someone I'm displeased with them I try doing it in a roundabout fashion, and only when we're alone.'

'How time-consuming!'

'Possibly. But it makes for pleasanter relations.'

'Then please treat me as a Thai!' she couldn't resist saying.

'I doubt if I can. I'm too intrigued by your difference.'

It was a compliment of sorts but it made her feel like a butterfly on a pin, impaled and examined by this commanding man who, in seconds, could veer from arrogance to teasing. He leaned towards her, one arm outstretched, and she drew back, then felt idiotic as his arm came past her to pick up one of her sketches.

'I noticed you wrote "embroidery" on a few.'

'Yes. But there isn't time to do it for this season. Deng gave me a book on your national costumes, and the handwork is wonderful.'

'Personally I prefer the embroidery done by our hill tribes.'

'I've only seen the materials they weave.'

'Then I'll take you into the hills and show you some—if you can spare a day away from here?'

'I can, but...' Her ridiculous habit of blushing brought a tide of scarlet into her face. 'It seems an imposition for you to have to do it. I'm sure Deng can take me.'

'You don't wish *me* to do so? I thought you enjoyed our day in Bangkok.'

'I did. It was wonderful.'

'Then allow me to repeat it.'

Excitement quivered through her but she was careful to hide it.

'It's settled, then,' he stated. 'And Deng can concentrate on getting the staff we need.'

Tansy could have kicked herself for thinking his offer had been prompted by personal interest, and kicked him even harder for not pretending it was.

'When are we going?' she asked coolly.

'I'm free on Thursday. It's a fair drive and we should leave by eight.'

The door closed behind him and she stared at it. It gave away as little feeling as the man who had just walked through it! Unaccountably she felt she had been skilfully manipulated, and wondered if it was possible to wriggle out of their date, ruefully concluding that once Vin made a decision it would be a major achievement to make him change it.

Yet why was she unwilling to go with him? Was it because their day in Bangkok had been *too* enjoyable and she was wary of repeating it? She was still ruminating on this when Ella Wainright sauntered in.

Always beautiful, she was given a warmer loveliness by the slight tan on her normally pale skin. She had obviously used Vin's absence to go on vacation. Or had they been vacationing together? Of course they had! How stupid not to have realised it. Ella had been in Phuket with him, probably sharing his bed while she herself had been indulging in foolish dreams.

'Hi!' the girl greeted her. 'I've come to see your sketches. Vin says they're fantastic, but I like making my own assessment.'

Tansy bit back the comment that only Vin's judgement was required, knowing that to say it was a declaration of war. Besides, Ella's father was distributing the clothes. Gritting her teeth, she indicated the sketches, watching as red-tipped fingers riffled through them.

'These are great, Tansy. I really go for the uncluttered line.'

'I may be including some embroidery,' Tansy felt obliged to admit.

'I know. Vin told me he's taking you to see what the hill tribes make.' Ella set down the sketches. 'Arunila's success is important to him because it means a lot to his father. If it weren't for that, he'd have closed the company long ago.'

'I'm grateful he didn't.'

'So am I!' Ella's smile disclosed small white teeth, vixen-sharp. 'But the man doesn't go with the job.'

'I beg your pardon?'

'Vin. He doesn't go with your contract.'

Tansy's breath caught in her throat, and it was a moment before she could speak. 'I find your remark most offensive. Vin is my employer—nothing more.'

'Then neither of us has anything to worry about.' Ella leaned against the desk, her shapely body outlined by faultlessly cut grey silk trousers and low-necked top. 'I'm sorry if I sound possessive, but Vin and I are serious about each other.'

The girl fell silent and Tansy fought a private battle. Painfully she conceded she wasn't impervious to her employer, and because of it had read more into their day in Bangkok than he had meant. Yet even as she thought this she knew she was letting him off too lightly. Damn it, he *had* flirted with her, not merely by look but by word.

'We aren't officially engaged yet,' Ella said into the silence, 'so keep it under your hat. Vin's parents are abroad and he's waiting for them to return before breaking the news.'

'I'm sure they'll be pleased.'

'Pleased he's finally settling down, but worried by his choice.'

Startled by the admission, Tansy showed it, and Ella's shoulders rose in a frustrated movement as she spoke again.

'They're worried in case I persuade him to settle in the States.'

'That's understandable.'

'I guess it is, and I'll do my best to reassure them. But it won't be easy. Vin's property empire stretches across the world and he can live almost any place that takes his fancy.'

Tansy couldn't envisage him living anywhere other than Thailand, but deemed it wiser to hold her tongue. Whatever Ella and Vin did was their affair.

All *she* was concerned with was making sure he didn't try to have an affair with *her*.

Thursday morning at seven found Tansy waiting for Vin in the lobby of the hotel, casual in a seersucker skirt and blouse, leather-thonged sandals on her bare feet. That should definitely tell him she hadn't gone to any trouble!

He hadn't either, she noted with chagrin as he stepped from a Jeep, muscular legs encased in denims, a T-shirt of paler blue hugging his chest. Lean he might be, but he had muscles of steel.

His 'good morning' was brief as she took her place in the front seat beside him. 'I hope you won't find the Jeep uncomfortable, but we'll be travelling on some pretty hairy roads.'

'Where are we going?'

'To Fang. Not too far from the Burmese border.'

'Isn't that the area they call the Golden Triangle, where opium is grown?'

'Unofficially grown. Cultivating poppies for opium was outlawed over twenty years ago, but regrettably it isn't easy to enforce.'

'Why not?'

'Because it's a large area and the terrain is wild— valleys and mountains and poor roads, if any at all. Often the only means of inspecting the land is by helicopter. The border police do a good job, but they can't do the impossible. Incidentally, the Emerald Buddha you saw in Bangkok was found not far from where we're going.'

Chiang Mai soon lay behind them as they headed north. Tansy had never driven in a car with Vin, and his handling of it personified what she knew of his character: firm control, and steady, relentless pressure. So would he conduct his life: always on top of a situation, pushing ahead with his ideas, brooking no arguments. It was disconcerting to feel she knew so much about him. Was it female instinct or had they met in another lifetime? Though she could count on the fingers of her hands the number of hours they had spent together, it was as if she had known him forever.

Dismayed at where her thoughts were taking her, she drew away from them, acknowledging the danger of allowing personal feelings to interfere with a commercial relationship. That was all that existed between them. Ella had made sure of that!

'The hill tribe you'll be meeting are the Yaos.' Vin brought her back with a jolt to the immediate present. 'They live in the mountains around Fang, and, like most hill tribes, came here from China or Cambodia in the last hundred years.'

'What are they like?'

'Clannish and shy, with a strong affinity to nature.'

'I'd be the same if I lived round here,' Tansy remarked, viewing the mist-covered mountains they were approaching. It was easy to appreciate why it was difficult to police this area, for there was no other road apart from the one they were travelling, which at best merited the description of indifferent.

'If the Government stamps out the opium trade, will it affect these tribes financially?' she asked.

'Unfortunately, yes, though they're getting every possible aid to grow other crops, especially new strains of tea. But it's hard changing the habits of a lifetime, and Fang's still a big centre for opium smuggling. On the positive side, tourism's a growing industry, though it's making the people greedy and turning the children into beggars. That's why I hope you can utilise the embroidery and weaving I'll be showing you. When my mother was younger she used to buy embroidered garments from the Yaos to sell in our shops, but Western women didn't go for the styles and we were left with them.'

'Do you still have them?' Tansy had the glimmer of an idea.

'Yes, about a thousand garments I think, stored in the factory.' The silky dark head inclined in her direction. 'I doubt whether even *your* talent can find a use for baggy wool trousers and embroidered smocks!'

She laughed. 'I wouldn't begin to try! But it may be possible to cut away the material and turn the patches of embroidery into belts or motifs on a dress. I assume the Yaos make everything by hand, and to get the amount we require could take a year, so using what you already have would bridge the gap.'

'Wait till my mother hears this!'

'I'm not promising anything,' Tansy said hurriedly. 'I have to see the things first.'

The smile he gave her was so warm she felt as if she had been touched by the sun. Watch it, she warned herself. This man is dynamite and can blow your mind! Deliberately she studied the view, and Vin was content to remain silent and concentrate on keeping the vehicle on the road.

As they climbed higher it grew bumpier, and Tansy gripped the sides of her seat in an effort to stop bouncing around like heating popcorn. 'Do you come here often?' she gasped.

'Not now, but frequently as a child. My father considered it important for me to explore rural Thailand. He was right too, for it's helped me keep my feet on the ground.'

'You're still a pretty high flyer!'

'But I haven't lost sight of what's important.'

'Which is?' Tansy was intrigued.

'Love of one's family, of nature and its conservation, and awareness that one should do more than simply make money.'

'You've done extremely well anyway,' she said. 'I don't mean it rudely, but——'

'It's a justified comment. But as long as my success doesn't come from stepping on others, my conscience is clear.' His jaw jutted forward. 'Sorry if I come across as a prig.'

'You sound nice,' she said impulsively.

'And you sound surprised by it!'

Tell-tale colour ran into her skin and his mouth curled upwards. 'Your habit of blushing is enchanting.'

'It's the bane of my life.'

'Why? Most men enjoy seeing a woman blush.'

'Only because it makes her seem the weaker sex,' Tansy retorted.

'Because it brings out the tenderness in a man,' Vin corrected. 'And with female liberation what it is, we get few opportunities to be tender.'

Tansy clenched her hands. Everything he was saying deepened her attraction to him, and she forced herself to remember that Ella had first claim on him. She bit back a sigh. He wasn't exactly flirting again, but his attitude towards her wasn't that of a man secretly engaged to another girl, and she had a strong impulse to confront him with it.

'And you?' Vin asked.

Startled, she glanced at him. 'Sorry, I was miles away.'

'I was asking about *you*. I've spoken enough about myself.'

'There's nothing to add to what I told you in Bangkok. I eat sleep and breathe work.'

'Doesn't marriage figure on your horizon?'

'The very distant horizon.'

She eased down her skirt, which had risen as she turned towards him and was disclosing too much silky thigh. The swift lowering of his head indicated he was not unaware of it, and the tilt at the corner of his mouth that he was equally aware she knew it.

'You sound as if you've had an unhappy love-affair,' he murmured.

'I've had no affair, unhappy or otherwise.' Too late she wished the words unsaid, for he pounced on them.

'That explains many things,' he said deeply.

'What things?'

'Your occasional nervousness. The barrier you sometimes erect around yourself. I sensed it in Bangkok.'

This was too much. She was no helpless female scared to death of men, and she wasn't going to let him think she was. 'I'm not in the least afraid of men, if that's what you're inferring, and I'm certainly not afraid of *you*.'

'"Afraid" isn't the word I'd have used.' A sleek eyebrow rose above the upper rim of his frames. 'I think "aware" of me is more apt.'

'Well, of course I am,' she said on a laugh. 'We're aware of each other. If we hadn't been, I wouldn't be under contract to you.'

'A good try,' he drawled, 'but that wasn't quite the way I meant that word—as you very well know.'

Tansy said nothing, and nor did he, apparently content to let his last comment speak for him. The skittering white clouds above them parted, allowing a shaft of sunlight to touch his face, and she studied it dispassionately, noting the determined chin, the smooth plane of his cheek, the golden bronze skin stretched taut over the bones. He was breathtakingly handsome, and confident to the point of arrogance. But it was more than this that frightened her. It was the cultural barrier, the differences of heritage, tradition and beliefs that could cause the great divide.

And that was not counting Ella!

A picture of the blonde American rose before her, and Tansy's anger against him intensified. Didn't he have any loyalty to the woman he had asked to be his wife, or did he consider himself free until his engagement was public record? And where did she herself fit into his scheme of things? As a pleasant interlude?

Her soft mouth firmed. All she was to him was an unknown quantity to be explored, a challenge to be conquered.

Like hell, I am, she thought grimly. Like hell!

CHAPTER EIGHT

As THEY approached Fang, Tansy was reminded of a Wild West town, Hollywood style.

'I keep expecting Wyatt Earp to gallop towards me!' she confessed, and Vin chuckled, slowing down to stretch his back and rub a hand across his nape.

'He wouldn't have been out of place here about thirty years ago. That's when oil was discovered here and they had a black gold rush. But it ran out fast, and within a few years everyone went home!'

They drove through Fang's main shopping street, and within minutes had left the town behind them and were climbing a dirt track up a tree-covered mountain.

'I did warn you,' he apologised as Tansy hit her head on the roof.

'I thought you were exaggerating!'

'In future, don't. I always say what I mean.'

Was this his subtle way of telling her he meant what he had said in Bangkok? She had no intention of asking him, nor would she have believed any answer he gave her.

The air grew colder the higher they climbed, and she was annoyed she hadn't brought a cardigan. But it was difficult to envisage being cold when you were sweltering in the heat, and she rubbed her hands down her arms to get rid of the chill.

'My jacket's on the back seat,' he advised. 'Slip it on.'

'I'm fine.'

'Don't argue.'

His tone was guaranteed to make her do exactly that, but coldness won the day, and reaching for his jacket—a soft blue suede one—she slipped it round her shoulders. Without putting her arms in it, she felt encompassed by his hold, conscious of the scent of the man emanating from the material.

As always she was uncomfortably aware of him physically, his leashed sensuality finding an answering response inside her that scared her to death. Not since her girlish fling with Tony Carey—a fellow student at college—had she experienced any sexual responsiveness, and she intuitively knew it didn't bear comparison with the response Vin could draw from her. There'd be nothing girlish about *that*, she mused percipiently.

His cool manner concealed passion, the heat of which could consume her unless she gave herself to it light-heartedly. Yet being light-hearted about love wasn't in her nature, and to fall for him would be disastrous.

'Feeling warmer?' he enquired.

'Much. But don't you need the jacket yourself?'

'A warm-blooded man like me?'

She trembled. He was laughing at her and she had to put a stop to it. 'Please don't flirt with me, Vin.'

'Who's flirting?'

The question could be taken two ways, and she was thankful when, at that precise moment, they rounded a bend and some twenty houses heralded their arrival at a Yao village.

Vin jumped from the Jeep and Tansy quickly followed, unwilling for him to lift her down. But she

wasn't able to prevent his hand coming under her
elbow to guide her towards the headman and his
family, who came out of his timber house to greet
them.

Vin chatted to him in dialect as he led them forward
to meet his wife and children, all of whom greeted
Tansy with sunny smiles and the traditional *wai*. The
mother and eldest daughter wore turban-style black
hats trimmed with bobbles of coloured wool, while
the heads of the remaining children were bare, their
hair black as night, their skin the colour of milky
coffee. They were all clad in multi-layered garments,
which was an excellent means of coping with the
changeable temperatures found at high altitudes.

There was no embroidery on their clothes, but as
the mother moved forward Tansy glimpsed scarlet and
green stitching beneath several layers of bodice, and
as the woman turned to say something to a child
behind her the baby on her back became visible, and
Tansy was entranced as much by its cherubic face as
the embroidered cap on its head.

Greetings over, they were *wai*-ed into a large room.
The floor was covered with rugs, and thin cushions,
serving as chairs, were set round a large, carved table
some twelve inches high. In the far corner a grate was
filled with logs, the only source of heat during the
sharply cold nights.

Dodging wandering chickens and a squealing piglet,
they followed their host into another room where two
girls sat at hand looms, behind them a long trestle
table piled with hand-woven cottons brightly embroidered with gods, serpents, flowers and temples.

As Tansy went to examine them, she noticed two
older women at a smaller table, sorting a mound of

coloured threads. 'Have these few women produced all this?' she whispered to Vin.

'Hardly! The village is a sort of a co-operative. Everyone works in the fields during the day, but any spare hour the women have, they weave and embroider—as well as spin the yarn and dye it.' His voice hardened. 'They have a tough life, and I hope we can find a market for all this.'

'I'm sure we can, now I've seen it. In fact I think we should show some ethnic clothes each season.'

Vin's pleasure was evident. 'Then our journey's been worthwhile.'

Worthwhile for these industrious tribes, Tansy thought sombrely, yet dangerous for herself, highlighting as it did the dangerous attraction she felt for a man who wasn't free.

'Do you want to freshen up?' he asked suddenly, misinterpreting her shiver of apprehension.

Hastily she nodded, and he spoke a few words to their hostess, who then ushered Tansy to a small room on the opposite side of the house. In the centre of its rough concrete floor was a hole, and beside it stood a small table holding squares of brown paper and a bowl of water. Her hostess *wai*-ed and withdrew, leaving Tansy to cope as best she could.

She stifled a wry laugh, thankful she had had insomnia last night and had spent the better part of it reading an amusing book on Thai customs, which had luckily included toilet habits. She'd have been in dead trouble otherwise!

When she rejoined the family she avoided Vin's eyes, mortified when he showed no such inhibition and sauntered over to apologise for not having asked their hostess to tell her how Thai lavatories worked.

'I hope you figured it out,' he concluded.

'Yes, thanks.' Resolutely she stared at the floor.

'You'll frequently find the same system in newly built homes,' he went on. 'Many Thais prefer it.'

Her colour intensified and she marvelled that a man who was usually infuriatingly perceptive where she was concerned didn't see he was embarrassing her. But in this she did him an injustice, for he unexpectedly touched her hot cheek with the tip of his finger.

'Unlike people in the West, we are brought up not to be shy of bodily functions.'

'I see.'

'Good. I don't want you thinking I'm trying to discomfit you.'

Oh, no, she thought, just trying to make me a second string to your bow! Not trusting herself to answer, she went over to re-examine the embroideries, remaining there until they were ushered back into the main room to eat.

The low table was covered with dishes of food, and everyone settled themselves on cushions around it, their legs tucked to one side. No risk of feet pointing at anyone!

The Chinese origin of these hill tribes was apparent in the food, which was a hundred times tastier than any she had eaten in her local Chinese take-away in London!

There was no cutlery, and she watched goggle-eyed as Vin curved his first three fingers into the shape of a scoop, and used it to pile his plate high with a little of everything. This was definitely her day for learning, she mused wryly, and proceeded to do the same.

After the initial shock of touching the food with her fingers, she enjoyed the experience, recollecting that as a child she had loved discarding her spoon and fork and using her hands.

During the meal Vin talked to everyone, and she noticed how nice he was with the children. Well, no one was all bad, she thought sourly.

'Sorry you can't join in the conversation,' he apologised. 'But you're doing a great job eating. From your first look of horror I thought you were going to pass out!'

'Shows how little you know me,' she retaliated, scooping up another portion of rice to stuff into her mouth.

It was early afternoon before they finally left. The family gathered around the Jeep to wave them goodbye, their hostess pressing a beautifully embroidered waistcoat into Tansy's arms.

'Don't refuse it,' Vin ordered under his breath, 'or she'll be hurt.'

Tansy gave the woman a warm smile, and for the first time essayed a *wai*. This was met with happy beams from everyone, and with waves all round Vin set the Jeep in motion.

'Next time you *wai*,' he commented as they bumped down the incline, 'put your palms closer together and only raise them to the base of your neck, not your nose.'

'What's the difference?'

'One of rank. The higher you raise your hands, the more respectful it is.'

'There are so many things to learn about your customs,' she grumbled good-naturedly.

'You're doing fine.'

She made no comment. She might be doing fine, but she still felt alien here. Except with Vin. The admission shocked her. After what Ella had said, she should be distancing herself from him, not feeling closer! Yet her attraction to him was so strong, and her response so instinctive that she couldn't control it. Fear trembled through her. Fear for her vulnerability, for his determination, and for where it might lead her.

She settled deeper into her seat, unexpectedly tired. The day had started early, and a bone-shaking drive was hardly conducive to relaxation, to say nothing of her verbal sparring with Vin and the tension his mere presence aroused in her. Gradually her lids grew heavy and she had to force herself to concentrate on the scenery. This was easy while they were bumping down the mountainside, but as the road levelled a little and became less rough, her lids drooped lower and finally closed.

When she opened them again, it was with a crick in her neck and stiffness in her limbs from lying in one position for—as a glance at her watch showed—an hour and a half.

'Sorry for being such poor company,' she apologised. 'I only meant to rest my eyes.'

'No sweat,' he shrugged.

His use of Western vernacular made him seem less foreign—which was not what she wanted. Opening her purse, she fished for her compact, more from a desire to occupy herself than a need to know how she looked. A flushed face stared back at her in the tiny mirror, and her deep blue eyes held a limpid, slumberous quality.

'Do you need reassurance that you're beautiful?' Vin questioned.

'Certainly not! Nor do I consider myself to be.'

'Then you're blind! You've an eye-catching body and pre-Raphaelite face and hair.'

'Do stop it!'

'You don't enjoy compliments?'

'I don't trust such lavish ones, and I don't like them coming from *you*.'

'Why not?'

'They're inappropriate.' She bit her lip. It was a less than honest answer, but the promise Ella had extracted from her obliged her to give it. 'Look, Vin, I came here to put Arunila on the map, and hopefully myself. But not if it means I have to be nice to you.'

With a jerk that would have sent her flying had it not been for her seatbelt, he stopped the Jeep.

'Do you honestly think the continuance of your contract depends on your being *nice* to me?' he thundered. 'That I'll use my position to get you into my bed?'

Expecting him to defend himself, Tansy was nevertheless startled by the vehemence with which he did it, and, since remaining at Arunila was important to her, she knew she had to back-pedal. Not enough to make him think he could carry on as he had been doing, but enough to soften the blow to his ego.

'I don't like being considered a sex object, Vin. I'd rather we stick to a business relationship.'

'You didn't give me that impression in Bangkok.'

She was on the verge of breaking Ella's confidence when he spoke again.

'It looks as if I've made the mistake of thinking you are as modern as your clothes!'

If by modern he meant promiscuous, he had another think coming. 'I believe in one man, one woman,' she retorted. 'I steer clear of men who have more than one string to their bow.'

'Naturally. A person who plays different tunes at the same time is hardly endearing!'

Did this mean he no longer loved Ella? If so, it didn't say much for the lasting power of his affections!

'I'm rushing you again,' he apologised. 'But it's hard not to when we're close and alone like this.' He edged towards her, his voice deep. 'Give me five minutes' grace and then I'll keep my promise to leave you alone, but right now I can't.'

Before she guessed his intention, he pulled her into his arms. The hard edge of the seat dug into her thigh, but she was more conscious of the heat and strength of his body and the firm lips pressing on hers. She struggled to free herself but was powerless in his hold, her head forced back by the unrelenting pressure of his mouth. Afraid of his anger if she fought him, she went limp. It was a clever move, for as she softened in his arms, his mouth grew gentler, the moist tip of his tongue stroking her lips as caressingly as his hands stroked the rounded curves of her breasts.

It was easy now for Tansy to draw away from him, yet she couldn't. The languorous warmth invading her at his touch rendered her powerless. Nor did she want to move, and with an incoherent murmur she raised her hands and clasped the back of his head. His hair was thick and soft as velvet, soft as the tongue invading her mouth. Desire pierced her, fierce as fire, sharp as an arrow, sweet as nectar, and she pressed closer to him, the tip of her tongue rubbing the side of his.

At its touch, he groaned deep in his throat and curved his hands intimately round her breasts, shaping his palms around their fullness to cup their weight. Skilfully his fingers undid the single button of her bodice, then did the same to her bra. Her breasts spilled free, swollen and heavy with desire, and his fingers rubbed the tender nipples until they hardened and rose, sending exquisite tremors shivering through her.

Oh, how she wanted him!

The suddenness with which he moved back from her left her defenceless, but the gentleness with which he smoothed away the damp tendrils of her hair from her forehead and straightened the bodice of her dress robbed her of embarrassment.

'I only asked for five minutes,' he whispered, 'and I always keep my word.'

Dumbly she stared at him. Keep his word? He certainly wasn't keeping it to Ella! What sort of man was he to spend ten days in Phuket with her and then blithely return to tell another girl it was all in the past? Even if he meant it, it was callous in the extreme, and if he could behave like that to one woman, he'd have no trouble doing it to another when it suited him.

'I don't want this to happen again, Vin.' Her voice was loud in the confines of the Jeep. 'I'm not saying it to play hard to get. I mean it.'

'But you responded to me.' He looked amazed. 'You can't deny that. We haven't known each other long, but ——'

'It mustn't happen again.'

'Why not?'

She drew a shuddering breath. To admit she knew he was secretly engaged would not only necessitate breaking her word but might give away the fact that she already cared enough about him to want more than he was willing to give.

'Let's just say I never mix business with pleasure,' she stared finally. 'If you can't accept that, I'll leave Arunila.'

'And break our contract? It will ruin your career.'

'I don't care. I feel very strongly about this. I find you attractive—I won't deny it——' how could she when she had just given him back kiss for kiss? '—but I don't want it to go any further, and since we have to work together, it's better if we stick to business.'

There was a lengthy silence before he broke it. 'If that's what you want, so be it. Friends, Tansy. Nothing more.'

CHAPTER NINE

PREDICTABLY Tansy spent a restless night reliving everything Vin had said.

Although she had threatened to break her contract, it would put paid to the chance of a lifetime, and Vin knew it, for he was too astute not to realise that had she been able to achieve success on her own she wouldn't have signed with Arunila.

This put him in the driving seat, and, remembering the dexterity with which he had handled the Jeep, she saw danger signs ahead. He had promised to leave her alone, but he wasn't the sort of person to accept defeat easily—regardless of what he had said. Indeed, her resistance to him could well be a challenge!

Miserably she pushed aside the single blanket covering her and went to sit by the window. Unlike in Bangkok, there were few lights visible at this ungodly hour, and the glimmer of street lamps did little to alleviate her unhappy mood. But as she sat there, shivering slightly in the cool air of night, her fighting spirit revived. She was damned if she would allow Vin to intimidate her. If the worst came to the worst she *would* leave, and if he sued she would plead harassment!

With mixed emotions Tansy entered her office next morning, but pleasure became uppermost when she saw what Deng had achieved in her absence. He must have worked like a demon to do so much in the space of twenty-four hours.

The two Australian models he had mentioned to her were waiting to be interviewed, and in the large room next to her office the seamstresses she had requested were sitting at the latest sewing machines, ready for action!

'You're a miracle worker, Deng!'

'I'm glad you think so.' His boyish grin made him appear younger than the twenty-eight she knew him to be. 'But we are expecting miracles from *you* and we must give you all the help you need. We'll all have to work like crazy to get the samples ready by mid-January.'

How right he was. Creating the designs was one thing, but turning them into finished garments was another, and she set about it immediately.

First the paper patterns had to be cut, and, after watching Arunila's two pattern cutters produce one from her most complicated design, she was happy to let them help her.

For five days the three of them were incarcerated in the cutting-room, working non-stop until every design was transformed into a pattern. Only then did they start making the *toiles*—copies of the actual clothes, but made in an inexpensive muslin-type fabric. This was done so that Tansy could amend her designs if necessary, and the pattern could be altered accordingly. Once this was done the garment would be ready to be made in the actual fabric.

It took the best part of three weeks for all the *toiles* to be completed, and Tansy was thankful to discover she only wanted to alter a few of them, which she was able to do by recutting the respective *toiles*.

'What's next on the agenda?' Deng asked, walking in on her.

'The most nerve-racking step of all—taking a pattern and cutting it in the actual material. But first I'd like you to arrange a little party for everyone who's worked with me these past few weeks.'

'You catch on quick,' Deng approved, rocking lightly backwards and forwards. 'I was going to suggest it myself. When do you want it for?'

'As soon as possible. I'd like to start producing our samples right away.'

'No problem. I'll fix up the party for late this afternoon.'

The festivities were in full swing in the sewing-room off Tansy's office, when Ella Wainright sauntered in. Tansy's pleasure evaporated like snow in a heat-wave—a good simile, she mused, for behind the girl's smiling face was ice. Did she perhaps guess that Vin was cooling off her?

'You're just in time to join the celebration,' Tansy said aloud. 'Tomorrow we start making the samples!'

'Great. The buyers are flying in on the first weekend in January and we have to start making the orders so they can be shipped out by mid-February. If they aren't, my father will skin me!'

The comment was light-hearted, but Ella's face was intent and, seeing her anxiety, Tansy warmed to her. Strange to feel that way about a rival! Yet they weren't rivals in the real sense of the word. As far as she was concerned, Vin could go jump in the lake!

'We'll be working flat out,' Tansy said aloud. 'If things go according to plan, we'll meet the deadline.'

'Good. Arunila's success means a lot to Vin.' Ella's coral-tipped hand reached for a sticky coconut cake, which she nibbled delicately. 'I can't stand this gooey stuff, but if I don't enter into the party spirit they'll think me rude.'

'I act the same at a cocktail party,' Tansy confessed. 'I can't stand canapés, so I put one on a plate and nurse it till I leave!'

'Seems we have something in common,' Ella smiled, surreptitiously dropping the remains of her cake into a waste-paper basket. 'Incidentally, if I can be of any help, let me know. I'm staying in an apartment in the same block as Vin.' Taking some paper from her purse, she scribbled a telephone number on it and gave it to Tansy. 'I'll be in Phuket with him for the next ten days, but I'm free any time after that.'

The cup in Tansy's hand shook. So much for his declaration! The man was nothing but an expedient liar.

'Vin's company and Jefferson's—his Australian partners—are putting up a shopping mall there,' Ella went on, 'and Vin wants to see how things are going.' She paused, her pale blue eyes roaming Tansy's face. 'Hey, you're pale as a ghost. You upset about something?'

Discomfited, Tansy desperately searched for a reason. 'I—er—I loathe shopping malls,' she lied. 'They're huge and soulless.'

'I think they're fantastic. Dozens of shops all easily accessible and under cover.'

'I shouldn't think being under cover is important in Thailand.'

'You won't say that in the rainy season! Nor when the temperature's in the high 90s. Air-conditioned malls are a boon.'

'I suppose I'm basically against turning one city into a replica of another. If we do, there'll be no point travelling abroad.'

'Aren't you over-dramatising the situation?' a male voice questioned, and Tansy raised her eyes and saw Vin standing by the buffet table. 'Shopping malls make life easier for shoppers, which is good for business, and therefore the economy of a country. They're fast becoming a part of modern living, and if I can ensure their architecture fits in with the landscape, I'll feel I've made a worthwhile contribution to society.'

'As well as to your property company,' Tansy couldn't resist saying, glad she was staring into black lenses, otherwise she might have been impaled by furious eyes.

Ella's ripple of laughter as she slipped her hand through Vin's arm robbed the moment of tenseness. 'Watch out, honey, it's unwise to quarrel with the key person in Arunila.'

'Tansy won't let personal considerations interfere with business,' he replied calmly. 'She's too level-headed.'

Tansy's urge to fling her coffee in his face nearly gave the lie to that, but she managed to keep a smile on her face as they moved off to chat to Deng.

It wasn't until they had gone that she was able to relax, and she was pouring herself another coffee when Vin spoke her name directly behind her, causing her hand to shake and to splatter hot liquid on her wrist.

Instantly a white handkerchief was wrapped around it, and she hurriedly pulled back. 'It's nothing,' she protested.

'Scalding liquid——'

'It wasn't that hot. I was startled more than anything.'

'By me? I'm sorry. I'd never wish to cause you pain.'

What a laugh, Tansy thought. He had come closer to causing her more pain than anyone else in her life, but at least it hadn't taken her long to discover his baseness.

'What do you want?' she asked, her voice steady, her heart thumping wildly as she resisted an insane impulse to touch his silky black hair.

'To say I'm sorry I won't be with you over Christmas.'

She looked at him blankly. Gracious! She had forgotten it was only six days away. She had air-mailed gifts to her family and then resolutely put the festivity to the back of her mind in case it made her homesick.

'I had planned to spend it with you,' he continued.

Astonishment held her spellbound. Had he intended putting Ella in hibernation? Honestly, the man was insane!

'I'll be far too busy to take any time off,' she said. 'I'll be lucky to get away from the factory for Christmas dinner at the hotel.'

'You can't carry on working non-stop. Tell Deng to engage more staff.'

'I'd still have to watch over them.'

Vin shook his head irritably. 'Any chance of bringing over your work-force from England? The samples you gave Mrs Gray were beautifully made.'

Tansy nearly laughed in his face. He'd collapse if he knew *she* was the 'work-force'! 'I'm afraid all my staff have gone to other jobs,' she lied.

'A pity.'

'I won't let you down, if that's what's worrying you.'

'*You're* worrying me, not the damned business.' He came a step closer to her. 'Have you forgotten our day in the mountains and what I said to you?'

'Hardly,' she said with a dry laugh. 'But I didn't take it seriously. My career is the only thing I care about.'

'One day I'll put that statement to the test,' Vin declared, and, turning on his heel, walked out.

Tansy unwound the handkerchief from her wrist and clenched it tightly. What sort of fool did he take her for? Ella had made no secret of their going to Phuket, yet he continued to maintain he was interested in her. He was either incredibly conceited or believed she was an idiot emotionally. Yet there was a third reason too, and he had practically stated it just now.

As head of a vast empire which happened to include Arunila, he could well believe that, rather than jeopardise her future as a designer, she'd be willing to fall at his feet.

Some hope he had!

Tansy was glad when the party was over and she was free to return to the Rincome. Deng refused to let her call a cab, and insisted on taking her himself.

'Don't let Ella pressurise you about the samples,' he said as they drove towards Chiang Mai. 'She enjoys laying down the law, given half a chance.'

Deng was rarely critical, and Tansy was surprised. 'You sound as if you've had a set-to with her yourself.'

'I haven't. But only because I'm careful to avoid one!'

'Have you known her long?'

'A year—since I came to work for Khun Vin. She was over here searching for high fashion clothes to import to the States. She met our handsome boss and—I'm sure you can guess the rest! I think it's because of her that he decided to revitalise Arunila by engaging a top designer.'

So that was what had motivated Vin! Keeping the company going for his father's sake was eyewash! He had done it to keep his affair going with Ella! Except that it was no longer an affair but a secret engagement. Or was it? In view of his pursuit of *her*, Tansy found it hard to credit that he'd ever marry the girl.

'I hope you'll have a good rest tomorrow?' Deng ventured as they reached the hotel.

'I doubt it. I'm too het up. I'll take it easy when the samples are done and the buyers have voted for them with their cheque-books!'

'By then you'll be preparing for next season.'

Her cornflower-blue eyes glowed with amusement. 'If that's the price of success, I'm happy to pay it.'

'By having no personal life?'

Accustomed by now to these kind of intimate questions, Tansy didn't fob Deng off. 'When you're determined to get to the top you can't spare the time for personal attachments.'

'But a happy private life makes you better able to cope with work. You can easily afford to relax and enjoy yourself, Tansy. No one's waiting to try to get your job, and Khun Vin is too pleased with you to let you go.'

Too pleased, and too intent on conquering her, Tansy reflected, but kept the knowledge to herself.

'So relax a bit,' Deng reiterated.

'Why? Hard work never harmed anyone—as my father's always saying!'

'Mine too.' Deng's wiry frame shook with laughter. 'Parents are the same the world over!'

Tansy was still smiling at this when she entered her room. A slip of paper on the floor informed her there was a package for her at Reception, and she called them to send it up, mystified as to what it was.

Sight of the cylindrical parcel deepened her curiosity, and tearing aside the wrapping she unrolled several sheets of architectural drawings. It was only when she saw a note from Vin attached to the last one that the mystery was solved.

'Simply to reassure you that not all property developers are philistines,' he had penned.

After perusing the drawings, she was obliged to agree. No concrete and steel complex here, but a modern version of an old Thai city. Stepped-roof houses and Buddhist-style temples incorporated shops and restaurants, while paved courtyards—set among lawns and palm trees—provided ample areas for shoppers to relax. Remembering her condemnation of the project, Tansy knew she owed him an apology and, without stopping to think, dialled his office number.

Only as she heard the telephone ring did she realise it was close to seven, and she was on the verge of hanging up when his voice came over the line.

'It's Tansy,' she blurted out. 'Thanks for sending me the drawings. I owe you an apology.'

'I didn't send them to you to prove you wrong, but because I wanted you to know I don't put profit before aesthetics.'

'I'm glad.'

There was nothing else for her to say, yet she was reluctant to end the conversation. I'm nuts, she thought. He's going to Phuket with Ella and here I am hanging on to his every word like a besotted schoolgirl.

'That's all I rang for,' she said stiltedly. 'I don't want to disturb you any more.'

'You can't help disturbing me, Tansy.'

Her hands grew clammy, and she answered with pretended naïveté. 'You've no cause to worry about me. I'll be so busy I won't have time to miss my family over Christmas.'

'I'll be busy too, but I'll still miss you.'

She shook with anger. Next thing he'd be telling her was that he and Ella were just good friends!

'Doesn't my missing you mean anything?' he asked.

Tansy hesitated, then took the plunge. 'I'm sure Miss Wainright will fill the gap admirably.'

'Ella's only coming with me to meet Jefferson's, my Australian partners,' Vin replied blandly. 'Her father's interested in joining some of our ventures and wants her opinion of their top directors. Like you, she's brainy as well as beautiful.'

'I got where I am without the backing of an important father,' Tansy couldn't help retorting.

'Then be proud of yourself—not jealous of another woman.' His voice softened. 'This isn't a conversation for the telephone. If I didn't have a mass of paperwork to go through, I'd come over to you.'

'I'm too tired to see anyone. In any case, we've nothing to discuss.'

'Hearing that tone of yours, I'd say we've a great deal to discuss. There's——'

'Have a good trip, Vin,' she cut in. 'And Happy Christmas.'

She replaced the receiver smartly, only then realising how silly her last remark was, for Christmas meant nothing to the Thais. Still, because of the tourists, all the large stores and hotels played Christmas songs and sported paper decorations, so her good wishes to him weren't so out of place.

What *was* out of place was disclosing her jealousy of Ella, for it would make him—despite the promise he had given her in the Jeep—more determined to continue his pursuit of her.

Fear prickled her skin. Could a gazelle outrun a panther? Had a vixen ever turned on a hound? A fly on a spider? Pacing the room, she caught sight of her worried face in the mirror. Blast Vin! She'd show him she was no push-over. She had controlled her response to him in the Jeep—well, almost—and she could go on doing so. Or could she?

Stumbling to a chair, she collapsed into it. She had told Deng she was ready to sacrifice her personal life to her career, but was she prepared to sacrifice her morals too, by disregarding Ella's position in Vin's life?'

'Never!' she cried aloud. 'If he won't take no for an answer, I *will* break my contract.'

Hearing herself speak lent strength to her assertion, and only then did she relax. Returning to England meant returning to the struggle she had hoped she had left behind, but it was preferable to being number two on a philanderer's hit list!

CHAPTER TEN

TANSY'S conversation with Vin so perturbed her that for the rest of the week she worked at a killing pace, making her personal seamstresses do the same.

Willing though they were, their standard of workmanship was nowhere near hers, and inevitably she lost her temper with them.

'How many times must I tell you not to set in a sleeve like that?' she snapped, lifting up the bodice one of the girls was sewing, and ripping out the offending item.

The girl lowered her head and remained mute, which inflamed Tansy the more until she caught Deng's eye and saw him frown. Muttering under her breath, she stalked into her office.

'You'll have trouble with the girls if you tell them off in public,' Deng warned, following her in.

Tansy, whose temper was as quick to abate as it was to rise, was ashamed of herself. 'You're right. It's just that I'm worried sick the samples won't be ready for the buyers.'

'They will. I've spoken to the girls and they're prepared to work until eight each evening.'

'How fantastic. When will they start?'

'Tonight.'

With the girls' working overtime, the rail of finished samples in Tansy's office grew fast, and she lost some of her tension. If there was no unexpected disaster, in a matter of weeks she would be sitting in the conference room at the Rincome Hotel watching the models parade ... It was enough to make her weak at the knees.

She took off Christmas Day, which she spent resting, and had Christmas dinner in the hotel. She deeply missed her family and, finding it impossible to enter into the party spirit, retired early to her room.

She had half expected a call from Vin, and concluded he hadn't felt it diplomatic to phone one girl while bedding another. All sorts of unwanted images flashed before her and she could happily have boiled him in oil!

She was staring morosely through the window when the telephone rang. She went weak at the knees. It was Vin, she knew it, but to hell with him! It rang again, and reluctantly she reached for it.

'Is that you, darling?' her mother cried.

For the next fifteen minutes Tansy and her family regaled each other with their news, and when the call ended she was lonelier than ever. Tears were pouring down her cheeks when a bell boy delivered a small package.

'Sorry is late,' he beamed. 'Came early but sent wrong room.'

Thanking him, she perched on the bed and unwrapped it to find a narrow leather box containing an exquisite silver and gold necklace. The baroque style was exactly her taste, but who was it from? Only as she lifted the wrapping paper again did she notice the folded note stuck to the underside. With shaking fingers she unfolded it.

'I'm sorry I cannot give you this personally,' Vin had penned, 'but I will enjoy thinking of you wearing it, and wish I were as close to you as the necklace will be.'

He was never lost for the right turn of phrase, she mused sourly. Did he think a beautiful gift could help her forget he was spending ten days with Ella?

Slapping the necklace into its box, she stuck it in a drawer, wishing she could do the same with Vin! Would the dratted man never give up, or was he so used to conquests that he couldn't accept a rebuttal?

On the first day of the New Year the bulk of the samples were completed, and she and Deng were sorting through them in the afternoon when Ella walked in, emanating the glow of a well-loved woman.

Tansy was appalled by the jealousy that engulfed her, but managed to greet her without showing it, relieved when Ella instantly focused on the crowded dress rails.

'These are out of this world, Tansy! The buyers will fall at your feet.'

'I hope you're right. What day are they actually arriving?'

'Next Saturday. We'll let them amble round during the day, give them dinner and a sample of Thai dancing in the evening, and show them the collection on Sunday.'

'We'll be taking the clothes to the Rincome on Saturday morning,' Deng interpolated.

'How many models do you have?' Ella asked.

'Our two regulars, and three more.'

'Good. Everything's going so well, the gods must be smiling on us.'

Tansy moistened her dry lips and forced herself to ask the question expected of her. 'Did you have a good trip?'

'Sensational. The men from Jefferson's are exactly the type my father will go for. Young, businesslike, aggressive and macho. He'll enjoy dealing with them. I know Vin does.' Ella glanced at her watch, muttered she was late for her hair appointment, and left.

Alone with Deng, Tansy sighed with relief. 'I'm glad she liked the samples.'

'I never doubted she would. I bet she's rushed to tell Khun Vin.'

Afraid Deng was going to discuss the couple, Tansy picked up her bag and disappeared through the door, using the same excuse as Ella!

The purple bloom of dusk softened the hard outline of the factories as she left the compound in search of a *tuk-tuk*, and it wasn't until she almost knocked into a tall, slim figure that she recognised it as Vin.

The unexpectedness of the encounter left her defenceless, all barricades down, allowing free access to the rush of joy which swamped her as she gazed into his bronze face.

I love him! she acknowledged despairingly. This isn't just a physical attraction. I really love him. Subconsciously she must have realised it the moment she had met him again in Chiang Mai, but had stupidly hoped that if she refused to acknowledge her feelings they would disappear.

But now she knew they wouldn't—knew too that he must never find out. If he did, he would lay stronger siege to her and she might cave in. The outcome would be disastrous, for she wasn't the type to love lightly, and when he left her for pastures new he would take her heart with him.

'I was coming to see you,' he stated, standing close.

'The collection's completed. I'll come back and ——'

'You are pleased with it?' he interrupted.

'Very much.'

'Then I'm satisfied. I'd much rather see *you*.'

'I'm going to the hotel.'

'You are in a hurry?'

'Yes.'

'You are meeting someone?'

It was dangerous to utter an outright lie and she shook her head. 'No, but——'

'Then please have dinner with me.'

Her throat constricted. 'I—I'm tired, Vin.'

He didn't move a muscle yet she sensed his displeasure. 'It will make me happy if you say yes,' he said formally.

Yes to what? Pushing aside the question, she nodded compliance, and he led the way to his white Porsche.

It was the car he had driven the night she had seen him with Ella in Bangkok, and the picture it brought to mind intensified her anger against him, making her stop dead and glare up at him.

'Don't you think you should be taking Ella instead?'

'She's busy,' came the smooth reply and, angrier than ever, Tansy slipped into the front seat.

Mutinously she made no conversation as they drove, but he didn't appear to notice her silence, nor did he break it as he parked the car and ushered her into Pat's Tavern Grill.

She was disconcerted by his choice of restaurant, for it reminded her of McDonalds, though the food, when it came, was considerably more up-market. The fillet steak she ordered was excellent, and the jacket potato—unlike others she had eaten in Thailand—was freshly cooked. Happily she made a mental note to come here whenever she was homesick.

'I like this place,' she said, making an effort to be sociable.

'I figured you might. That's why I brought you here. I had an idea you were pining for home.'

His accurate assessment put her on the defensive again. How awful if he guessed the other emotions raging inside her!

'Deng's been marvellous,' she rushed into speech. 'He's always there when I need him.'

'It's what he's paid for.'

The flat comment warned her that Vin probably saw her in the same terms: as a talent he had hired and could dispose of if it didn't suit him. He no doubt ran his personal life in the same manner.

A waiter placed another fresh mango juice in front of her, and sight of the gold chain round his neck reminded her of Vin's present.

'Thank you for your Christmas gift. It was lovely and very unexpected.'

'When I saw it, I instantly thought of you—elegant and beautifully made.'

'What a pretty compliment. Thanks.'

'I mean it.'

'Do you always mean what you say?'

The black lenses glittered in the light. 'I mean what I say to *you*, though there are several things I *can't* yet say.'

She shook her head, auburn curls tumbling. 'You've lost me, I'm afraid.'

'One day I'll explain it to you.' He set down his fork, but left his hand, long and slim, resting beside the plate. 'I've found you a house to rent. I think you'll be happier there than in a hotel.'

'Oh, I will!' Dislike him though she did, she couldn't restrain her pleasure. 'How long can I rent it for?'

'It's available for six months. It belongs to an American friend of mine who's gone to New York. There's a live-in housekeeper who will take care of you, so you won't have any work to do, nor will you be alone at night. We'll go and see it after dinner.'

'What's the rent?'

'Minimal, and Arunila will pay.'

His tone brooked no argument, and she didn't give him one. After all, why look a gift horse in the mouth? Excited to be moving into a place of her own, Tansy was impatient until they were cruising along a wide road on the outskirts of the town, with Vin slowing down every so often to peer into the darkness.

'It's further out than I remembered,' he muttered.

'Haven't you been here before?'

'Once. We generally meet in town.'

He drove on a little further, then stopped. They got out, and Tansy saw a sturdy-looking house on stilts, a row of wooden steps at the side leading to the front door.

'It's a typical Thai home, as you can see,' Vin said.

'I thought you only built houses on stilts if they were near water.'

'There are other reasons too. It keeps out wild animals and snakes.'

'You're joking!' She peered into his face. 'Aren't you?'

'As far as this house goes, yes. But let's go inside before we're attacked by polar bears!'

Laughing, he caught her hand and pulled her up the flight of steps. She felt they could be an engaged couple house-hunting, then hastily pushed the notion aside as they slipped off their shoes and he unlocked the door and ushered her into a large living-room.

It had a homely, lived-in atmosphere. The wood floor was polished to a patina, the same careful attention given to the beautifully carved items of furniture: low tables, bookcases, and a long sideboard housing the obligatory stereo, TV and video. There were also two comfortable sofas and armchairs in beige leather, and the soft radiance of table lamps illuminated several colourful Thai paintings.

Tansy didn't hide her pleasure, and without embarrassment followed Vin into the bedroom, noting the king-size divan, and fitted cupboards.

'There's a bathroom leading off it,' he explained, opening another door to show a modern bath and shower. 'And on the other side of the living-room there's the kitchen and domestic quarters.'

'It's perfect. I was fed up staying in a hotel.'

'If I'd known, I'd have done something about it earlier.'

'I doubt that,' she said without expression. 'You wanted to be sure you liked my designs first!'

He swung round on her. 'Does that clause still annoy you?'

'Not especially. In your shoes I'd have done the same.' She returned to the living-room. 'It's a stroke of luck this house being vacant.'

'Tom and Siri live in New York six months of the year.'

'Poor things! I'd loathe such a yo-yo existence.'

'I'm not sure Tom and Siri like it either, but they had to work out a compromise.'

Unexpectedly, Vin ensconced himself on a sofa, long legs stretched out in front of him, giving Tansy no option but to perch on a chair, careful to keep her distance from him.

'Tom met Siri when he came here to research a book, and when they married he didn't give a thought to the consequences of transplanting her to Manhattan.'

'I take it she didn't like it?'

'On the contrary. She went overboard for it! What she didn't like was living away from her family.'

Oh, yes, the family, Tansy thought. Supremely important to the Thais. 'What happened?' she questioned.

'Tom moved here. From a writing point of view he can work any place.'

'So why spend half the year in the States?'

'It was Siri's idea.' Vin's mouth softened, drawing attention to the sensuous lower lip. 'Being a dutiful wife, she considered it wrong to cut her husband off from *his* family.'

'Then they'll continue commuting?'

'Things may change once they have a family of their own!'

'Do you approve of mixed marriages?' Tansy was horrified to hear herself ask this question. But it had loomed so strongly in her mind since he had started talking about his friend that it had slipped out.

Not in the least disconcerted by the question, Vin pursed his mouth as he considered it. 'I can't give you a simple answer to that, I'm afraid. It depends on the countries involved, and the personalities of the couple.

There's a similarity between all Far Eastern peoples, but between East and West the differences can lead to many problems.'

Tansy had not expected such a careful answer, which was silly of her, for Vin was not the type to give an opinion lightly.

'If a Western man marries an Eastern or Far Eastern woman, the difficulties can be less,' he went on. 'Even if the woman has a career, being a dutiful wife is inculcated in her. But if an Eastern *man* marries a *Western* woman there's likely to be trouble. She'll expect to have an equal say in everything pertaining to the marriage, as well as consider it her right to do her own thing!'

'I should think so too!'

He laughed. 'I knew you'd say that.'

'But these friends of yours,' Tansy went on quickly. 'If Siri is dutiful, why didn't she try harder to get used to living abroad?'

'She did try, but Tom knew she was unhappy.' A mischievous smile creased the narrow, bronze face. 'Besides, all women—whatever their nationality— know how to nag!'

'A typical male comment!' Tansy expostulated. '*I* don't nag.'

'I imagine you have more interesting ways of achieving what you want.'

The intimacy of his comment charged the atmosphere between them, and Tansy was not only suffocatingly conscious of Vin's body but of her own. Her breasts swelled and her nipples grew erect, pressing against the soft fabric of her bodice. There was a tremor in her stomach and an ache of desire inside her that made her long to fling herself into his arms and experience the touch of his hands and mouth.

Across the room they gazed at each other. She wasn't aware of him moving but suddenly he was beside her, pulling her back with him on to the sofa until she was lying full length, and he was lying beside her, hard chest against the softness of her breasts, hard loins pressing on her thighs but mouth soft as it covered her own, parting her lips with the pressure of his tongue, to probe and dart into the inner sweetness.

Later she would regret her response, but now she revelled in it, knowing this was all she could allow herself, all she would have to remember him by. With a soft moan she clung to him, and, sensing her acquiescence, he brought his hand up behind her back to skilfully lower the zip of her dress. As it fell away from her body, he drew back slightly to look at her. A vein beat visibly in his temple and the sheen of sweat on his forehead showed the control he was exerting on himself.

She longed to remove the heavy glasses, desperate to see the expression in his eyes. After all, it wasn't bright in here, and surely there was no danger in just a moment's breaking of the specialist's rule? But as her hand rose, his rose first, not to remove the heavy frames but to unclip her bra and let the fullness of her breasts spill their softness into his waiting palms. Tenderly he clasped them, his fingers lightly teasing the nipples. They hardened instantly, twin peaks of throbbing ecstasy that set up the same fire between her legs. She trembled and moaned again, a more urgent sound this time, and he responded by lowering his head and drawing one nipple into his mouth.

Aflame with longing, she shakily began undoing the buttons of his shirt. Impatiently he pushed her hands away and tore the shirt open, and she ran her fingers across the satin smoothness of his skin. It was golden brown and soft as velvet, except where it was roughened by a splattering of dark hair. Touching her lips to it, she breathed in the warm muskiness of him, drawing it deep into her lungs and wishing it could enter every part of her body.

'I want you,' he said thickly, and, tilting her head up, brought his mouth down hard on hers.

It was hard and hungry with desire and she responded to it blindly, twining her slender legs around his muscular ones and revelling in the throbbing muscle which surged against her inner thigh. Its insistent pressure awakened her to the danger of what could happen and, suddenly panic-stricken, she pushed at him.

'Vin, no!'

Ignoring her plea, he trailed his mouth down the side of her neck to the shadowy cleft between her breasts, then lower to the soft velvet of her stomach. The moist tip of his tongue probed the hollows, but as his fingers lifted the edge of her silk panties, she gripped his hand.

Instantly he was motionless, then he slowly raised his head to look at her. 'I only want to touch you,' he whispered.

Had Tansy believed he loved her she would have revelled in his need, but because of Ella she felt besmirched.

'What are you afraid of?' he asked.

'Of you, of myself,' she answered with partial honesty. 'I'm an old-fashioned girl, Vin, as I've already told you, and I don't go in for affairs. When I give myself to a man it will be because I'm going to marry him.' She felt his body stiffen, not with passion but shock.

'Are you saying...?' He paused. 'You are a virgin?'

Her cheeks grew hot but she refused to lower her eyes. Dammit, she wasn't ashamed! 'Yes, I am. I can see you're surprised.'

'Very. It isn't unusual here, but for a Western woman...'

'I suppose it would do your ego good to be the first?' she snapped.

'More than my ego, Tansy. Knowing I was the first man to enter you, the first to whom you had given your heart and your body, would be a memory I'd cherish all my life.'

Tansy trembled. His answer would have satisfied the most critical woman, and she was heartbroken that it had come from a man who would never think of her in terms of marriage. Indeed, her very use of the word was now bringing him to his feet, and he was moving away from her, leaving her free to sit up and hastily put on her bra and dress.

'One day you *will* give yourself to me,' he said deeply.

'Never.'

'You say this because you are jealous of Ella?'

To answer 'yes' would give herself away, and instead she managed a credible laugh. 'Much as it may astonish you, I don't want you.'

In the act of buttoning his shirt, he stopped dead. 'After the way you responded to me, I find that hard to credit.'

'I don't see why. You're an experienced man who knows a trick or two, and I enjoyed you! But I don't want a repetition.'

To her fury, he flung back his head and laughed. 'I like your sharp tongue, Tansy. I can see you'll never bore me. But I don't believe a word of what you've said.'

'Time will prove I mean it.'

'Really? I might prove the contrary.'

Not deigning to reply, she went to the front door.

As they left the house the silvery brightness of the moon was covered by a cloud. To Tansy it was symptomatic of her personal life, and she knew that somehow or other she had to find the emotional strength to forget Vin as a would-be lover and see him merely as a stepping-stone to her successful career in the fashion world.

But oh, how impossibly difficult it was going to be!

CHAPTER ELEVEN

WITH the buyers arriving the following weekend, Tansy decided to move into the house next morning, and within a couple of hours was packed and en route to her new home.

Entering it for the second time, she found it even more welcoming than on the first occasion, and was sorry she hadn't thought to move from the hotel long before, regardless of whether Arunila would have paid. Had she lived in home-like surroundings she might have been less unsettled mentally, and better equipped to cope with Vin.

But it was pointless thinking of the might-have-beens. It was the present which concerned her, and, recollecting what she had said to him last night, she knew she had dealt with him in the best manner possible.

As she set her cases on the floor, a Thai woman of indeterminate age glided into the room and introduced herself as Ampa. Her English was passable, for she had worked for Westerners for seven years, and she assured Tansy there was no necessity for her to bother herself with any domestic chores.

Cognisant of the work ahead of her, Tansy was happy to hear this and, wandering into the bedroom, savoured the anticipation of waking up each morning to see the snow-capped mountain peaks from her window. And who wouldn't be tempted to sing with a twinkling waterfall in the garden below, where cicadas and multicoloured birds filled the champagne air with trilling sounds? It was heaven whichever way you looked at it!

Thrilled with her new home, Tansy found she was also better able to cope with Ella, who had taken to visiting the factory every day. Sight of her was a constant reminder of Vin, though even if Ella had not been on the scene she doubted if she could have blocked him from her mind.

'These clothes are so fabulous I'm going to have several for myself,' Ella stated one afternoon as she walked the factory floor beside Tansy.

'Priority goes to the buyers,' Deng grinned, overhearing her. 'Business associates take second place!'

'I'm practically family!'

Tansy averted her head. Did Ella know how Vin felt about Eastern men marrying Western women, or was she confident of overcoming his prejudice? As a wife she was unlikely to be dutiful, though her keen business brain would go a long way towards making the marriage happy.

Murmuring that she had things to do, Tansy returned to her office and sat blindly at her desk, trying to convince herself her misery would diminish with time. She had fallen in love with Vin quickly and there was no reason why she shouldn't fall out of love equally fast.

'I'll be glad when the collection's shown and Ella stops hassling me,' Deng declared from the threshold. Unusually for him, his black hair was mussed and he appeared irritated.

Tansy kept a diplomatic silence, knowing he was perfectly capable of standing up to Ella. He might seem easygoing but there was more strength to him than met the eye.

'You know the venue for the show is changed?' he continued.

'No, I didn't. Where to?'

'The Makram home. Khun Vin's parents have returned from the States two weeks earlier than expected, and want it to be held there.'

Well, that was one way of meeting Vin's family, Tansy acknowledged, though she wished it had occurred when she was in a more relaxed frame of mind. Fat chance! When Vin was near her, she was tense as an overwound spring.

The arrival of the two Australian models and the three European girls Deng had had flown in from Paris gave Tansy no opportunity to think of anything other than the business in hand, and the next two days were spent deciding which girl should model which outfit, choosing the accessories to go with each one, and placing them in a muslin bag attached to the relevant dress hanger.

The buyers were jetting in at noon on Saturday, and Vin and Ella were meeting them at the airport. Tansy, unable to face the sight of the two of them together, had pleaded pressure of work and managed to opt out, though she felt obliged to join them all for dinner later.

She refused to think beyond this point, aware that her career depended on the outcome.

Was that why Vin had kept his distance these past few days? To lessen his embarrassment if the show flopped and he terminated their contract? Or did his absence indicate his acceptance of her rebuttal, and signify he wasn't going to waste further time on her?

She prayed it was the latter reason, and, despite assuring herself it was better if they didn't meet, none the less longed to see him.

On Friday night she was so beset by nerves she could only toy with the dinner Ampa had prepared for her, and she was pushing her food round her plate when Vin telephoned. It was clear from what he said that Ella had kept him informed how everything was progressing.

'You sound distant,' he declared after they had spoken for a moment.

'It must be a bad line.' Deliberately she misunderstood him.

'Distant as in cool, Tansy.'

'Sorry. I suppose I'm edgy.'

She expected him to say she was worrying for nothing, as Deng and Ella had, but he remained silent. She had every reason to be on tenterhooks, and it wasn't in his nature to give false comfort. Yet when he did speak, she realised she had done him an injustice.

'Any profession that appeals to public taste is a nerve-racking one, Tansy, and creative people are always putting themselves on the line. That's the negative side of having talent. The positive is that they have a gift which nourishes their lives.'

Tears brimmed in her eyes. How clearly he understood the pain and pleasure of creativity. It made it all the sadder to know he could never be part of her life except in the business sense. Yet could she bear to stay in a job that brought her into frequent contact with him? She had asked herself this many times since falling in love with him, but wasn't sure of the answer.

'Are you there, Tansy?'

His voice was soft in her ear, almost as if it were caressing the lobe, and she shivered, despising herself for wanting a man who was warming another woman's bed. 'Yes, I'm here. I was just mulling over what you said and—and you've made me feel better.'

'I'm glad. Try to get some sleep. I'll see you at the dinner tomorrow.'

Saturday morning she went to the factory and watched the samples—each shrouded in a cotton cover—hung on racks and rolled into a van to be transported to the Makram home. Deng refused to let her go with him and his assistant, advising her to take the day off and relax.

'I hope you're wearing something sensational tonight?' he asked.

'One of my designs, what else?'

Only when the laden van had departed did Tansy leave the factory.

Eschewing the tourist-filled shops, she decided to visit Wat Prathat, the temple that perched on the top of Doi Suthep, the most prominent of the mountains ranging the city. Her taxi passed rice fields and skirted the zoo—which housed some of the wild animals still found in the region—before climbing the twisting hairpin road to deposit her at the foot of the steps leading to the temple, one of the most famous in the region.

Staring up at them—two hundred and ninety in all—she thought she must be crazy, and with a rueful smile began to climb. She was breathless by the time she reached the top, and paused to catch her breath and peer down on Chiang Mai, a thousand metres below. It resembled a toy town and she tried to believe it was, and everyone in it toys too. But Vin refused to be cut down to size, and loomed as large in her thoughts as if he were beside her.

Turning from the view, she crossed the cloister and entered the temple, leaving her shoes by the door where others had piled theirs. As she sat cross-legged on the floor, the peace of her surroundings gradually worked its magic, and she remained there for more than an hour, allowing the prayer-soaked atmosphere to seep into her bones.

She was considerably calmer when she returned home, and she showered and rested before dressing for dinner. She had been joking when she had told Deng she was going to wear something sensational— her preference was to be as inconspicuous as possible. But the advantage of being eye-catching was obvious, and Vin would have every right to be annoyed with her if she wasn't.

After careful perusal of her wardrobe, she donned flowing trousers in jade silk, which gave the impression of a skirt until her graceful walk showed otherwise. It was topped by a figure-hugging short jacket in Thai style, buttoned high to the throat, the material a mixture of jade and the same deep blue as her eyes.

The matching of Western and Thai design symbolised the clothes the buyers would be viewing tomorrow, and Ella, darting from one group to another, was quick to notice it as Tansy entered the suite Arunila had booked at the Rincome to entertain their visitors. The girl also sported a dress in Thai silk, though it had the stamp of Paris, and was a reminder to Tansy of Ella's moneyed background.

There was no sign of Vin, and she gave a visible start when he spoke her name behind her. Swinging round, she found herself so close to him that his breath was warm on her cheek. In a dark suit, with pale tie, he was every inch the conservative tycoon. Heavy black frames still partly concealed his face, giving him a Machiavellian air.

'All this must be very boring for you,' she said, then could have kicked herself at his look of surprise.

'If something is important to me, it isn't boring. And Arunila's success *is* important.'

'But it's such a small part of your empire.'

'Size doesn't necessarily equate with significance, as you'd know if you studied astronomy!'

'Aren't you ever lost for an answer?'

'Rarely. Though occasionally I don't give an honest one!'

'You once told me you always meant what you said,' she couldn't resist replying.

'I was referring to anything I said to *you*.'

She was still searching for an answer to this, when he spoke again.

'You must circulate, Tansy. We'll introduce you to the buyers.'

It wasn't a royal 'we', she found, for with Ella on his other side they wandered the large room, greeting the three-hundred-and-fifty-strong contingent who had flown halfway across the world to see the Arunila Collection. There were many famous names among them, and Tansy prayed she would justify Diana Gray's faith in her and Vin's financial gamble. A mixture of fear and elation swept through her. She was on the threshold of a wonderful future—providing she didn't fall flat on her face!

Tansy remembered little of the evening, beyond constantly smiling and endeavouring to say the right thing, but her appearance brought many compliments, though none from the one man from whom she wanted them. But then with Ella beside him he had to be careful!

Two glasses of wine helped her to sleep through the night, and amazingly clear-headed she awoke to a dawn chorus of birds and sprang out of bed to breathe in a lungful of the clear, champagne air. She loved this time of day when everything was fresh and cool. Yet she loved the sunny days too, when puffs of fleecy white clouds chased each other across the pale blue sky. But then she enjoyed everything about Chiang Mai—or was it because she was near Vin and could look forward to the bittersweet pleasure of seeing him?

Angrily pushing aside the thought of him, she donned a pencil-slim sleeveless dress in silver-grey. It was a shade rarely worn by anyone with her colouring, but Tansy's unerring eye knew it gave lustre to her tumbling auburn curls. Deliberately she pulled her hair away from her face plaiting it into a thick braid before looping it in a low coil on the nape of her neck. It emphasised her high cheekbones and drew attention to her large, jewel-blue eyes, shimmering with apprehension. It was this give-away emotion which made her unpin her hair and shake it loose again, allowing the curls to camouflage the apprehension her stark face had disclosed. She might be scared, but she had no intention of letting the buyers know it. In all business, confidence was the name of the game.

Deng collected her at seven-thirty, smart in a pale grey suit, his black hair slicked smooth, and they left the city from the north west corner—the same road she had travelled yesterday. But today they were going several kilometres further, for the Makram home was situated in the hills near the King's summer palace.

As they climbed higher the air grew fresher and the scenery more lush than any she had seen in England. How far she was from her family on this momentous day in her life. What if her designs were an almighty flop? Fear gripped her and she rushed into speech, afraid that if she didn't she would panic.

'I didn't realise the Makram home was so far from town. Does Vin live with his parents?'

'Officially.' Deng's swift glance was all-encompassing. 'He has an apartment in Chiang Mai, which he frequently uses.'

I'll bet! Tansy thought sourly.

'But he's spending more and more time abroad,' Deng went on, 'particularly since linking with the Jefferson Company. They have many building projects in Australia and the States.'

'I can't imagine his having partners. I think he prefers doing things *his* way.'

'The Jeffersons let him! He decides on the projects and venue, and they control the building works. There may be a few changes now old man Jefferson has handed the reins to his son, but Ella was very impressed with him when she met him in Phuket. She says he's as strong a character as Khun Vin, and won't let him have things all his own way.'

Tansy was intrigued that Ella had spoken so frankly to Deng, and assumed he had asked her. It was Thai curiosity again! Yet strangely enough they were also a tactful race, restraining their interest in you if they sensed their questions would hurt.

From the window, she saw they were approaching a private estate protected by a high wall. Imposing gates were guarded by a sentry who inspected them carefully before allowing them through. Once inside, the lush wilderness changed to carefully tended lawns, and flower-beds bursting with orchids, hibiscus and flaming bougainvillaea.

They bowled along a tree-flanked drive for half a kilometre before the Makram home came in view. And what a home! More of a palace at first sight, with its colourful tiled roof and ornate façade.

A manservant hurried forward to open the car door, and, leaving their shoes on the wide veranda which ran along the entire frontage, they entered a vast, marble-floored hall. It was sparsely furnished but the few pieces—long, narrow table in the centre and carved chairs set against the walls—were antique and beautiful.

Many doors, all closed, led off this area, and with a *wai* another servant ushered them through a series of rooms—all sparsely yet magnificently furnished with antiques and statuary—before leaving them in a room of ballroom size, its windows overlooking a view of undulating mountains.

Gilt chairs were ranged in rows either side of a newly erected catwalk in the centre of the room, and Deng crossed the teak floor, masked here and there by thick, hand-woven rugs, to a door at the far end.

Following him, Tansy found herself in a smaller room filled with dress rails, models chattering and setting out their make-up and hair pieces, dressers agitatedly taking garments from their covering bags to check the accessories, and seamstresses doing last-minute alterations.

As expected, Ella was much in evidence, alternately smiling and hectoring. Not that Tansy was complaining, for with so few women here experienced in showing a collection she needed all the help she could get.

For the next few hours, the two of them went through the running order, checking the lists to ensure each model would be wearing the dresses earmarked for her, and that she had all the accessories for them.

Inevitably there were minor crises: a belt was missing from a jacket, and was finally found attached to a dress; there was an inexplicable grease mark on the hem of a skirt, which caused hysteria before it was finally expunged, and the music tapes weren't with the tape deck, and a driver had to be sent to Chiang Mai to fetch them.

The choice of music had almost precipitated a row between Tansy and Ella, for the American girl had wanted the models to gyrate to the strong beat of Sting, while Tansy had felt her clothes would be best served by a more melodic sound. She had stood firm, determined to go to Vin if necessary—what a pickle it would put him in, having to adjudicate between the girl he was secretly engaged to and the one he secretly lusted after!—but luckily Ella had caved in.

Now, as Ella watched the models do a quick rehearsal in time to a Sinatra ballad, she came over to Tansy and flung out her hands in a supplicating gesture.

'Next time I'll know better than to argue with the preferences of the designer,' she grinned.

As always, Tansy was taken aback by Ella's warmth towards her, then reminded herself that as the girl had no idea Vin was trying to two-time her she had no reason to be otherwise.

Shortly before noon the buyers arrived, and Tansy headed for the back room, where she intended staying until the show was over.

'At least come and have a drink with them first,' Deng urged, rushing in to find her. 'And Khun Vin's parents want to meet you.'

'Later,' Tansy gulped.

Recognising obdurateness when he saw it, Deng left, but hard on his heels Vin sauntered in.

'If you've come to get me out of here, forget it,' she flared.

'I only came to wish you luck.'

His tone was mild, his manner easy, and confidence oozed from every pore. A grey tusser suit hung faultlessly on his tall, slim frame, his skin glowed with vitality, and there was a golden hue to his tan that she had never noticed on the faces of other Thais.

He has it all, she thought bleakly, and wondered if she was foolish not to be part of his personal life even if only for a short while. At least it would give her wonderful memories! But she dismissed the notion instantly. 'Love 'em and leave 'em' was not her philosophy, and being Vin's lover when he was also Ella's would be utterly degrading.

'I'm sorry I didn't invite Diana Gray to come here today,' he said. 'It might have made you feel better.'

'Or worse,' Tansy said through dry lips. 'She'd have insisted on a preview, and if she'd hated——'

'Enough! I won't listen to such nonsense.'

He leaned towards her and she tensed. If he kissed her she would scream—or else passionately return his kiss—either action being disastrous! But he merely touched her forearm and went out, leaving her staring after him with bleak eyes.

CHAPTER TWELVE

TANSY remembered little of the next two hours. She knew she helped the dressers prepare the models, and that she went on checking the accessories, but it wasn't until Deng was pulling her on to the catwalk amid thunderous applause that she knew the collection was a triumph.

Like bees to a honey pot, the buyers converged on her, and she was embraced and kissed, and had her hand shaken until it went numb. In an amazingly short while the order book was full, and Ella excitedly waved it in front of her before dashing off to appease an irate owner of a department store who wished to double her original requirements.

'How does it feel to be the toast of three hundred and fifty of the world's top buyers?' Vin had quietly come to stand beside her and, buoyant with success, she beamed at him.

'Too wonderful for me to analyse. I just want to wallow in it!'

'You'll be doing a lot of wallowing from now on. But time enough to talk business later. First, I wish to introduce you to my parents.'

Nervously she followed him as he forged a path for her towards an elderly couple standing by a window. Anxious to show she was no ignorant foreigner, she *wai*-ed them, palms together, fingers uppermost, forehead lowered respectfully.

Vin's mother was tiny and narrow-boned, her face ivory-skinned and unlined, her hair black except for two wings of grey at the temples. His father was darker-skinned and resembled a jolly Buddha, only slimmer, with grey-streaked hair and heavy-lidded black eyes. He was fairly tall, as were most Northern Thais, though Vin topped him by a head. To her consternation, no sooner had he introduced her to his parents than he was called away, leaving her to converse with them alone. Their gentle questions soon put her at ease, and when Vin's mother asked her what she thought of the hill-tribe embroidery she had seen, Tansy launched into her plans for it.

They were discussing this when luncheon was announced, but instead of joining everyone on the shade-covered terrace, where a forty-foot-long table was spread with a lavish buffet, the Makrams stood aside from the mêlée and motioned Tansy to do the same.

'We are still suffering from jet lag,' Vin's mother said, 'so we are lunching by ourselves. But we will very happy if you will join us.'

'I'd like to,' Tansy said, 'but Vin may be expecting me to mingle with the buyers.'

'I think your work is done for the moment,' Khun Ungart, Vin's father, stated, and with the insistence of authority gently motioned her to follow them.

Tansy found herself in a small room on the other side of the house. It overlooked a less tamed garden, the flowers and shrubs giving the impression of growing free, which she found very much to her taste.

On a dais in the centre of a room was a low table with cushions around it, and they ensconced themselves here while two servants glided in and set dish after dish upon the table, until it was covered with silver bowls, each filling the air with a delicious aroma.

'Have you had a *Khantok* dinner before?' Vin's mother enquired.

'No, I haven't. Is it a special kind of food?'

'Yes, and a special table too! *Khantok* means wooden tray. Its shape is always round and it's made of teak and has five legs—like the one we're sitting at. Years ago people ate from a mat on the floor, but then a Buddhist monk in Northern Thailand made one of these tables, and once everyone saw how convenient it was to put their food on it it became a standard piece of furniture. In honour of the monk who devised it, we now have a special "*Khantok* dinner", though Westerners usually find it too spicy.'

As if on cue, two more servants carried in further silver dishes of curry, fried noodles, Chiang Mai sausage—a special blend of minced meat—a bamboo basket filled with sticky rice, and a silver salver on which lay steaming-hot napkins.

Following the lead of her host and hostess, Tansy used one to wipe her hands, then manfully picked up her chopsticks and began eating. The food was spicy, no arguing with that, but it was absolutely delicious.

The Makrams continued to ply her with questions, mainly regarding her background as a designer, and Tansy—now she had proved she was truly a successful one—was more honest in her replies, admitting that lack of capital had prevented her achieving success in London.

'A few months ago we believed Arunila was finished,' Khun Ungart informed her, 'but your brilliance has saved it.'

'Thank you for saying so, but even without me your son would have kept the company going. He knows how much it means to you,' Tansy assured him, deciding the lie was justified.

Husband and wife glanced at one another conspiratorially. 'I wonder if we may share a little secret with you, Miss Simmonds?' the man ventured.

'Of course.'

'I've been playing a subtle game with my son. You see, keeping Arunila going was never important to me.'

'It wasn't? Then why did you want him to think it was?'

'For selfish reasons,' Vin's mother put in softly. 'He has so many projects overseas that we wanted him to concentrate on one here. We felt it was a good way of making sure he doesn't—how you say?—grow away from us.'

Knowing the regard in which Vin held his family, Tansy couldn't envisage this happening. 'I think you're worrying for nothing. Vin's so attached to his heritage and culture, I can't see him being happy to live abroad for any length for time.'

'It's always possible,' his father replied. 'Other customs and beliefs can insinuate themselves into your life without your being aware of it, and the more Vin travels, the greater the chance of his making his home elsewhere; especially if he falls in love.'

'With a Westerner' was implicit in this comment, and Tansy appreciated why. But she didn't understand why she had been the recipient of the Makrams' confidences, unless they believed that, as a Westerner herself, she was privy to Ella's future plans.

'You're all very deep in conversation.' Vin's melodic voice made the three of them turn.

'We're getting to know this gifted young woman,' his father answered with commendable aplomb.

'That was the purpose of the exercise,' Vin grinned and, leaning forward, caught Tansy by the arms and pulled her to her feet. 'You've been indoors too long. A walk in the garden will do you good.'

Barely giving her time to thank her host and hostess for lunch, he steered her into the garden, and away from the house.

'Of all the cheek!' she exploded. 'I was enjoying myself with your parents.'

'It's time *I* enjoyed myself, and I can only do that with *you*.'

'Am I a court jester as well as a dress designer?' she snapped.

'How sharp you are,' he chided. 'You've obviously had a harrowing day.'

It was more harrowing to have him close beside her, but she dared not admit it, and strolled on.

'I missed not seeing you this week,' he continued.

'You're a busy man.'

'And going to be busier for the next few months.'

'There's no necessity for us to meet,' she shrugged. 'The collection's behind us, and all we now have to do is start delivering the orders.'

'Why do you enjoy deliberately misunderstanding me, Tansy?'

She stopped walking and angrily faced him. 'You're the one who's misunderstanding. I've made my feelings for you abundantly clear but you still continue harassing me. I'm not interested in you, Vin. Can't you get that into your head?'

'No, I can't.'

Before she could stop him, he pulled her into his arms and pressed his mouth hard on hers. Tansy struggled to free herself, but his hold was too tight and she was trapped; nor did he raise his mouth from hers, kissing her harder the more she struggled, until the painful pressure of his lips on the soft inner flesh of her mouth made her gasp.

As her lips parted, his tongue instantly found entry. It was not soft and gentle as it had been once before, but fiercely probing, asking—no, demanding a response she was determined to withhold. But his onslaught continued, and one muscular leg pushed between hers and threw her off balance, causing her to fall and bring him to the ground with her. Or maybe he had planned it this way? Whatever, they were lying together on the soft grass, hidden from sight by thick flowering bushes. With his body covering hers and making her escape impossible, he was able to free his hands, and they roamed her slender curves and full breasts as if by touch alone he could slake the desire burning in him.

'I need you,' he grated deep in his throat. 'I haven't thought of anything else for weeks.'

'Not even Ella?' The words were torn from her.

'She means nothing to me. Forget her.'

'The way you've forgotten you're engaged to her?'

'What?'

'Don't bother lying.' Fury shattered Tansy's control, breaking the promise she had made. 'I've known about it for weeks.'

'I see.' As if in slow motion, Vin eased his body away from Tansy's. 'I take it she told you?'

'Yes.'

'I have never asked her to be my wife,' he said flatly.

'Really? Did she imagine it, or simply assume it from your behaviour? You *have* been quite close with her, wouldn't you say? And still are, from the way she acts towards you.' Tansy's anger escalated, and she sat up. 'Ella doesn't *behave* like a girl who's been jilted. But then she hasn't been, has she? You want both of us, don't you?'

'No!'

'Great! Because you aren't getting me. Three in a bed has never appealed!'

'I'm not asking you to go to bed with me,' he said swiftly. 'Just to wait till——' He broke off, his mouth moving convulsively, perspiration sheening his forehead. 'Listen, Tansy. I want you more than I've wanted any woman in my life, but I daren't upset Ella, and——'

'Then don't! Keep her forever, for all I care!'

'You've got it wrong! Listen to me, Tansy. Her father's the biggest importer of our clothes. It would be madness for me to part enemies with her. All I'm asking is for you to give me a bit more time.'

'So you can go on prostituting yourself?'

He jerked back as though she had hit him. 'I don't have any choice. I'm in a tricky situation and I can't let my personal feelings sway me.'

For an instant Tansy closed her eyes so she would not see his face. He was worse than she had imagined. She might have forgiven him had he said he couldn't hurt Ella, but to admit he was remaining her lover because of Arunila not only showed contempt for the girl, but for herself too.

Cynically, she acknowledged that many men in a similar position would do the same, but she had not expected it of Vin. It was not so much a question of moral rectitude as emotional fastidiousness, and she was appalled to think he didn't have any.

Would he behave similarly with women of his own nationality? Having met his parents, she doubted it, and this not only increased her anger, but also her pain. Had he ever considered *her* as a wife, he would never have humiliated her by asking her to wait until it was no longer expedient for him to be Ella's lover.

'I know you're upset, and I bitterly regret it,' Vin said into the silence. 'That's why I hadn't planned on telling you how I felt about you until I was free. But when I'm near you I want you so desperately I can't think straight. All I'm asking is that you wait for me.'

'For how long? Weeks, months?' Staring into his face, Tansy longed to rip off his glasses and see his eyes. Yet it was better she couldn't, for what she saw there might be worse than she imagined.

'Probably months,' he said slowly.

With a great effort Tansy made her voice amused. 'Honestly, Vin, I've never heard anything so silly.' She chose the word deliberately, hoping to show him she wasn't taking him seriously. 'I was simply testing you to see how low you'd stoop. Even if you ditched Ella here and now, I wouldn't have you. You see, I love someone else.'

'You're lying!' Vin's hands were steel bars on her shoulders as he dragged her hard against his chest. 'You're lying because you're hurt.'

'It's the truth.'

'Then why didn't you tell me before?'

'It was none of your business.'

'Well it *is* now. Who is it?'

Annoyed that her unruly tongue had run away with her, she wildly searched for an answer. 'It's the—the bearded man you saw me with at the Oriental Hotel last September,' she said with a flash of inspiration.

'The bearded man?' Vin echoed, clearly not remembering.

'Yes. We were going to marry but he—he changed jobs and it meant we'd be constantly travelling round the world. I wasn't willing to give up my career, and we quarrelled about it.'

'But you still love him?'

'Very much.' She forced a break in her voice, not too difficult when she was already on the verge of crying. 'If I could turn back the clock, I'd act differently.'

'I see.' Vin rose, smoothing his shirt, and running a hand over his hair. 'After what you've said, I'm amazed at your response to *me*.'

Trust him to spot that! Hurriedly she sought for a reason. 'When you held me I—I was so desolate I tried to make myself believe it was him.'

'Which you did very successfully.'

'I know, and it's made me realise that being with the man you love is as important as having a career.'

'I'm glad I was of service! I hope things work out for you.'

'So do I.'

'Don't forget you're under contract to Arunila, Tansy.'

It took her a second to follow his meaning. 'What will you do if I walk out on my contract?'

'Try it and see.'

'Don't worry. I've more integrity than you! I'll stay here providing *you* stay out of my personal life. I know we have to meet to discuss the company, but that's all.'

She sped across the grass and, once out of his sight, paused in the shade of a tree to tidy her dress and reapply her lipstick. One thing was definite. Remaining in Thailand long-term was out. She had to find a means of designing for Arunila without living here.

Fixing a smile on her face, she returned to the house.

CHAPTER THIRTEEN

Tansy breathed a sigh of relief when the buyers finally left Chiang Mai. She had spent the entire Monday with them while they enjoyed another day of sightseeing and lavish meals which Arunila had laid on for them, and the sight of Ella queening it had irritated her to screaming-point.

Yet it was hard to fault the girl's behaviour to her, for she was lavish in praise of her work, and expounded on her talent to each and every buyer she pigeon-holed.

Vin only put in an appearance at the dinner on Monday evening. He was polite to Tansy, but the hard line of his jaw as he spoke to her showed he was still infuriated by their altercation of yesterday. What gall he had to consider himself outraged when *she* was the one who had been insulted!

The effort of maintaining a pretence of normality throughout the evening gave her a migraine that kept her wakeful through the night. She was prone to them, and in moments of stress they returned. This one, when it finally abated, left her so exhausted that she took Tuesday off, and rang Deng to apologise.

'There's no fun being the boss if you can't take a day off when you fancy,' he assured her, his soft voice, with its faint American drawl, helping restore her equilibrium, and reminding her not all men were as callous as Vin.

For the rest of the morning she lazed in the garden beneath the shade of a flaming-red jacaranda tree. Ampa kept popping out to see how she was, and to reassure the woman she wasn't yet dying Tansy had a light lunch and went into town.

Avoiding the shops, she wandered round the market stalls. How beautiful these people were: gentle and unassuming and going about their business with as little aggression as butterflies. Many of them resembled butterflies too, their colourful cheongsams vying with the merchandise spilling over on to the pavements.

Enjoying the bustle, and feasting her eyes on the food carts, cheap jewellery and colourful parasols, Tansy succumbed to the lure of a vivid scarlet and green one, then bought several as gifts to send home. Goodness knew when there'd be enough sun in England to warrant their use, but they were pretty enough just to be admired.

Her purchases completed, she decided to treat herself to tea and cakes at the Orchid Hotel. It was modern but had many Thai features in the décor, including an abundance of carved wood, pagoda-style lamp shades, and the sparkle of gold everywhere, from gilded panellings to gilt ashtrays.

The coffee shop was less colourful than that at the Rincome, but the service was as friendly as she had grown to expect in this country. It was strangely pleasant to be by herself, and she experienced an unexpected sense of tranquillity. She would soon get over Vin. She had her whole life ahead, and she wasn't going to let him destroy it.

'Tansy!'

Her name rang out and she swung round to find a rangy blond giant loping towards her. Kevin? She stared at him in disbelief. The voice was his, as were the bright blue eyes, but the beard had gone, disclosing a solid jaw, and the wild hair was cut short and well styled. As for his clothes, they would have done credit to a Wall Street banker! A beautifully tailored suit in silk mohair drew attention to his well-muscled body, and feet she had last seen in thonged sandals were shod in Gucci loafers.

'What a stroke of luck bumping into you!' he exclaimed. 'You're the last person I expected to see.'

'Same here,' she greeted him, moving her bag for him to take the chair beside her.

'Another vacation?' he joked.

'I'm working here. And you?'

I'm working too—not here—I've flown in for a conference.' He shook his head. 'I can't believe we're really together. I've thought of you many times since our dinner in Bangkok, and kept kicking myself for not taking your address in London. I won't make the same mistake again. So tell me, how long have you been here?'

'Since October. I'm designing clothes. In fact I showed my first collection on Sunday and it went like a rocket!'

'I always knew you'd get to the top.' He leaned closer. 'You're as beautiful as ever, angel, but you've lost weight.'

'I'll take that as a compliment,' she smiled. 'Actually it's the heat and different food.' As an excuse it was admirable, and she made a mental note to use it again if necessary. 'But what's *your* news, and where's the hippy I once knew?'

'He's gone.' Kevin preened deliberately. 'Do you like my new image?'

'I liked the other one too!'

'I won't forget you said that!' His eyes twinkled and his curly mouth curled more as he beamed, showing that beneath the sophisticated façade he was the same friendly Kevin she had first met.

'Are you staying in this hotel?' he went on.

'No, I'm in a rented house. If you're free to come to dinner tonight——'

'I can't. My meeting may go on for hours, but I'll buzz you when I'm finished.'

Scribbling her address and telephone number in her notebook, she tore off the sheet and handed it to him. As he took it, he clasped her hand in his big one.

'I'm not going to lose touch with you again, Tansy. I haven't stopped thinking of you.'

'I bet you say that to all the girls!'

'Right. But with you, I don't keep my fingers crossed!'

She laughed, head thrown back, auburn curls cascading to her shoulders. It was only as she straightened that her eye caught the glint of shiny black lenses. Oh, no! Wasn't there any place in this town where she could avoid Vin? To make matters worse, he was striding in her direction.

Only then did she recall telling him she was in love with the man he had seen her dining with on her first visit to Bangkok. He had not remembered him, but what if the sight of Kevin jogged his memory?

'Kevin!' she whispered urgently. 'Whatever I say, go along with it, and don't look surprised.'

'What's the——?'

'I'll explain later.'

'Sorry to keep you waiting, Kevin,' Vin's melodious voice broke in on them. 'Or should I apologise for being too early?'

Bemused, Tansy glanced at the two men. My God! Vin was the man Kevin had come here to see! Yet when she had told Vin she was in love with the bearded man he had seen with her in Bangkok, he hadn't realised they were one and the same.

'You should have been an hour later, mate!' Kevin was saying to him. 'If I'd know Tansy was in Chiang Mai, I'd have been here months ago.'

The wide shoulders stiffened. 'You know each other?'

'Yes.' Tansy rushed in to take over the conversation. 'I told you about Kevin the other afternoon—in the garden—remember?'

'How could I forget?' Vin drawled. 'But you didn't say it was Kevin, and the face of your escort that night at the Oriental didn't register with me.'

Mystified as to what connection the two men had—Kevin was a geologist and might be surveying land for Vin—Tansy was still forced to brazen out the situation.

'I never thought I'd be seeing Kevin again, and I thought it might be awkward if you realised I knew him.' Aware that Kevin must be one big question mark inside, she caught his hand and half raised it to her cheek. 'You *have* forgiven me for putting my career first, haven't you, darling?' she asked meltingly.

'I'll forgive you anything, sweetheart, as long as you don't run out on me again.'

'Sorry to break the tête-à-tête.' Vin didn't sound the least bit sorry. 'But if we delay our talk, some of the directors won't be able to attend.'

'I can take a hint!' Tansy smiled, rising. 'I'll see you later tonight, Kevin.'

'Nothing will keep me away.'

With a man either side of her, Tansy left the hotel, pausing at the entrance.

'May we drop you somewhere?' Vin asked with cool politeness.

'No, thanks. I'm taking the day off and wandering round.' She glanced at Kevin. 'After the success of my first Arunila Collection, I'm sure my boss won't object to my having a break!'

This time Kevin did her proud, for though he must be astonished that she was working for the man she had once called arrogant and overbearing, not by the flicker of an eyelid did he show it.

'If things go as Kevin and I plan,' Vin spoke behind her, causing her to step back and regard the two men directly, 'you'll be working for both of us. Kevin's father, Luke, is not only interested in building shopping malls, but investing in our Arunila shops, too.'

Tansy had difficulty hiding her shock. Kevin Jay was Kevin Jefferson? The little lie she had spun on Sunday was threatening to engulf her. With a super-human effort she faced Kevin and, sensing her turmoil, he put his arm around her, the pressure of his hand indicating a promise to explain.

'Until tonight, angel,' he pledged, leading her past Vin to an empty cab. 'We'll talk later,' he whispered, helping her in.

She managed a smile and, conscious of Vin some yards behind, tilted her face to him. Instantly he bent forward to kiss her. She couldn't respond to it, but

he kept his lips on hers for a long moment before
drawing back.

Immediately Tansy waved the driver to move off.
Her sister's accident apart, this had to be the most
dreadful half-hour of her life.

The moon had turned the garden into a silver fairyland
when Kevin arrived at Tansy's house.

He had dined with Vin, but produced a splendid
box of chocolates and four bottles of Australian wine,
which she knew had cost him dear, for wines and
spirits were extremely expensive in this area of the
world, and served to remind her—if reminder was
necessary—that the fairly impecunious man she had
believed him to be was heir to the Jefferson empire.

Thanking him for his gift, she put three of the
bottles in the cupboard, and one in the refrigerator
to cool.

'Stop fussing around,' he ordered, 'and tell me the
reason for your lovey-dovey act this afternoon. I
assume it *was* an act?'

'Afraid so.'

She could never be more than friends with Kevin,
and it was wrong to give him false hope. Settling in
an armchair facing him, she briefly explained how she
had come to work for Arunila—that was the easy
part—but it grew more difficult as the emotional angle
intruded.

'I was in Bangkok visiting some of our suppliers
and Vin happened to be there too,' she went on. 'We
struck up a more personal friendship and it—er—it
sort of went on from there.'

'Understandable, sweetheart. In different ways
we're both gorgeous! So?'

'So he's also having an affair with Ella and asked me to wait until he breaks it off!'

'Wow!' Kevin's blond eyebrows rose high. 'I'd never have believed it of him. He'd have done better not to say anything to you until he was free of her.'

'I suppose he thought he could have us both at the same time! When he saw how disgusted I was, he changed his tune and asked me to wait for him.'

'It's a hell of a way to act.'

Tansy debated how to continue. It was less than tactful, in view of Kevin's and her business association with Vin, to say he was willing to prostitute himself with Ella because of her father's importance to Arunila, yet she had to give some kind of explanation.

'Vin felt it would be less hurtful to Ella if he—if he let their affair peter out, rather than end it abruptly.'

'You're kidding? I've heard of letting a girl down lightly, but that's crazy!'

'It's disgusting,' Tansy snapped, 'and I told him to get lost.'

'But how did I come into the picture?' Kevin asked.

'I—I needed a defence against him. You see, I . . . I love him. But he must never know. If he did, he'd keep pestering me and making my life a misery. That's why I had to give myself a cover, and I—er . . .'

'Told him you were in love with *me*.'

'Yes. I didn't say it was you straight off, but he asked me, and then I remembered he'd seen us together at the Oriental. I never dreamed I'd bump into you again, and of course I had no idea of your real identity. Vin didn't link my bearded hippy with

Kevin Jefferson, and I guess we both had a shock this afternoon!'

'Seems I owe *you* an explanation there.' Kevin ran a large hand through his hair, causing the flatly brushed waves to lift. 'My folks split when I was a kid, and my mother shortened our name to Jay when she took me to live in the States. I only saw my old man for a couple of weeks a year, and it wasn't until he had a heart attack a week after I left you in Bangkok that I went to Sydney to stay with him for a while. I guess you could say that's when I really got to know him, and I started seeing certain things from *his* side.' Kevin paused, his heavy sigh signifying regret for the wasted years. 'When the doctors ordered Dad to retire, he begged me to take over, and I agreed.'

'It makes a change from teaching English to a family with umpteen children!'

'It's more of a challenge,' he grinned. 'Dad says I'm doing a fair job, which in his terms is a great compliment! I'm also holding my own with Vin, and that's saying something, for he's a tough guy in business.'

'He's a tough guy, period,' Tansy retorted, and Kevin frowned.

'I can't believe what you told me about him, but if it helps you I'm happy to play your fiancé.'

'That's sweet of you, Kevin. I do appreciate it.'

'Being "sweet" relegates me to the "good friend" class,' he grunted. 'Maybe if I were a swine like Vin, I'd stand a better chance with you.'

'Never! No woman with any integrity could want a man who's willing to... Dammit! He's no better than a gigolo!'

The hurt she had been holding at bay surfaced, and she hurried into the kitchen, ostensibly to bring in the wine.

As they were sipping it, Kevin gave her a sheepish smile. 'You're going to hate me when you find out what I did this afternoon. You see, I figured you were playing up to me to make Vin jealous—I'd no idea it was more serious than that—so I suggested he and Ella have dinner with us tomorrow night.'

Tansy blanched. Having to pretend for hours that she was in love with Kevin and didn't give a damn at seeing Vin with Ella was a daunting prospect.

'I can't do it. You'll have to dream up an excuse.'

'Think of it as the hair of the dog. Seeing him with Ella may be cathartic.'

Tansy doubted it. Seeing him with Ella would intensify her jealousy, set fire to an imagination already working overtime. How easy to picture his magnificent bronze body entwined with the pale, slender one; the sensuous mouth devouring pink-tipped breasts as they had devoured hers. The glass trembled in her fingers, and Kevin gently took it from her and placed it on the table.

'If Vin's got to you this much, maybe you'd be wise to move on.'

'I'm under contract, and Vin says he'll sue me if I break it. If he did, I'd never get another job with a decent fashion house.'

'Then start on your own again. Jefferson's will back you.'

'Oh, Kevin! That's a wonderfully generous offer, but, if I accepted it, it would affect your relationship with Vin.'

'Then I'll back you personally, and no one need be any the wiser.'

'Thanks, but it's still no. I'm going to stick it out here.' Reaching for her wine, she took a fortifying sip. 'I won't let him destroy everything I've worked for.'

'That's my fighting Tansy,' Kevin exhorted. 'Remember, I'll be a shoulder to lean on.'

'When you're thousands of miles away in Sydney?' she joked.

'Even then.' He was no longer smiling. 'I can hop on a plane and be with you in a day. From the moment I met you I felt something special, and seeing you again has confirmed it.'

'Don't say any more,' she pleaded.

'OK. But don't forget what I *have* said.'

She nodded, regretting she couldn't have given her heart to this gentle blond giant, instead of a man who didn't understand the meaning of the word love.

CHAPTER FOURTEEN

NEXT day, Tansy managed to forget her forthcoming dinner with Vin and Ella by concentrating on work.

It had been impossible to fulfil all the orders they had received unless the factory worked two shifts, and Deng, with his usual speed, had arranged it. But then there was never any trouble finding staff in this country.

Walking into the factory after her day of rest, she was conscious of the charged atmosphere, the bustle of activity reflected in the increased numbers of garments coming off the production line.

'You're a miracle man, Deng!' she exclaimed, not for the first time.

'Let's say I was sufficiently confident of your success to recruit everyone we needed weeks ago!'

'Bless you for it!'

Impulsively she kissed his cheek. He flushed and she instantly apologised, aware that Thais didn't show such affection in public. Indeed, she had been amazed to see men walking hand in hand, though Deng has assured her this was no more than a normal sign of friendship. But the 'greeting' kiss, as practised in the West, was unheard of here, and the usual gesture of affection was to place one's mouth against the side of the other person's neck and breathe in.

'You may kiss me any time,' Deng chuckled now. 'That's the advantage of working with a Western lady!'

'I probably will. Beats me how I'd manage without you.'

It wasn't until she returned home later in the afternoon that the horror of the coming dinner set her temples throbbing. It was going to take every vestige of her control to get through tonight without giving herself away. Only one good thing might come out of this evening. If Vin believed she and Kevin were close, he would leave her alone. She refused to consider what would happen if and when Kevin found himself a real girlfriend and put paid to *their* pretended affair. Time to worry when it occurred.

To bolster her confidence, Tansy donned a dress she had designed six months ago for a boutique that had gone bankrupt before collecting it! An intricate blend of blues and lilac, with a plunging neckline and a softly flowing skirt, it made her appear sexy yet ethereal, an air increased by keeping her hair loose and brushing it into a thousand riotous waves.

Kevin's stunned silence when he collected her was all the accolade she required, and she gave him a brilliant, artificial smile like the one she planned to use this evening.

'Where are we having dinner?' she asked as she settled back in their cab.

'At the Pagoda. It's a new place, Vin said. Chinese and sensational.'

Tansy relaxed. She had been scared stiff of going somewhere where she might have had to dance with Vin, but it was unlikely in a Chinese restaurant.

Oh boy, was she wrong! she admitted sourly as they entered the cool elegance of a marble foyer and she heard the soft strains of a calypso. Not only was there dancing here, but it was the 'hold me close' kind!

'Vin and Ella have beaten us to it,' Kevin whispered in her ear, and Tansy kept a fixed smile on her face as she walked towards their table.

A broad-shouldered man, with satin black hair and piercing silver-grey eyes, rose to greet them. Where was Vin?

'Good evening, Tansy,' said the man in Vin's voice, and she sank quickly on to her chair, afraid that if she didn't sit down she'd fall down! Vin with silver-grey eyes? Impossible! No Thai had eyes that colour; they were either black or brown.

Speechless with shock, she mumbled a greeting, thankful that Kevin's exuberance masked her consternation. Why had Vin let her believe he was Thai? Everything he had said to her had validated it: his defence of the Thai way of life, both religious and cultural; his continual references to 'my' parents, 'my' sisters. The more she remembered of their conversations, the more mystified she was.

'You look as if you've had a shock,' Ella drawled, her cool voice capturing Tansy's attention.

'I have,' Tansy agreed, knowing it was obvious anyway. 'It's the first time I've seen Vin without his mask.'

'Mask?' Kevin questioned, and Vin chuckled before she could reply.

'I think Tansy's referring to my aviator glasses.'

Tansy forced herself to look directly at him. He had resumed his seat and was leaning back negligently, one long-fingered hand toying with the stem of his wine glass. At close range his eyes were remarkable, the silver-grey irises rimmed by a fine dark line. Without the disfigurement of heavy-frames, his high-bridged nose was evident, the fine cut of his features more noticeable. Of course his skin was still olive and his hair blue-black, but he was definitely not Thai.

Tansy's gaze slid to Ella, who was animatedly chatting to both men. As usual, her dress moulded every curve and left little to the imagination. Happiness radiated from her, softening her hard-edged image and making her appear less brittle. Even without benefit of an important father, she was a girl many men would desire, and, despite the reason Vin had given for staying with her, Tansy bleakly decided he had been diplomatic rather than truthful.

Her eyes met and held the silver-grey ones. She ached to look away but stoically refused to give him that satisfaction. 'What's it like to see the world in colour again?' she asked lightly.

'As if I've been reborn!' His glance strayed to her hair. 'I pictured it exactly the colour it is. Wine-red.'

Ella, engrossed with Kevin, none the less heard this and tapped Vin playfully on the arm. 'What colour's mine?'

'Champagne,' he said suavely.

'A great idea!' Kevin agreed, giving the order to a waiter hovering near.

'We've such a lot to celebrate,' Ella beamed. 'I was telling Vin we should show your next collection in Paris. In fact, I think we should have a permanent showroom there.'

'Let's walk before we run,' he advised.

'We're *already* running!'

The arrival of the champagne curtailed their discussion, and as pale amber liquid frothed into goblets Kevin raised his high and caught hold of Tansy's hand.

'A toast to the best designing woman I know,' he announced, 'and my fiancée!'

Tansy almost choked. Was he mad? Or was this his idea of a joke? But joke or not, he had said it, and it was met with stunned silence. Ella's brightly painted mouth was half open, her eyes wide, but it was Vin who held Tansy's attention. His face was expressionless—he was too old a hand at pretence to give himself away—but she noticed a muscle twitching at the corner of his mouth, and the momentary clenching of one long-fingered hand on the stem of his wine glass. Poor Vin. He didn't like losing his prey!

'What a sly puss you are!' Ella exclaimed to her. 'Vin was just telling me you and Kevin knew each other, but I'd no idea it was *so* well.'

'To your happiness,' Vin interjected. 'I hope this doesn't mean you intend stealing our star, Kevin?'

'Funny you should say that, mate. I'm working on it!' He gave Vin a playful punch on the arm. 'Seems to me Tansy can design equally well from Australia, and there'd be no sweat about her flying back for meetings or staying here while the samples are being made.'

'I doubt it would work as easily as you make out,' Vin countered. 'Tansy's the catalyst that's set Arunila bubbling, and we can't afford to let the company off the boil! Her presence works magic.'

'For me too,' Kevin murmured, his adoring gaze making it evident he would sooner or later return to the subject of her moving to Australia.

Tansy returned his gaze with one equally adoring. If anyone could get Vin to change his mind, it was Kevin. After all, they were partners in such huge financial ventures that Vin wouldn't want to do anything to sour their relationship.

Kevin clasped her hand again, and glancing down she was startled to see him sliding an exquisite ruby ring on her engagement finger.

'Almost the colour of your hair,' he murmured, drawing her hand to his lips.

His face was suffused with such tenderness that her heart went out to him. A short while ago she hadn't believed he could care for her after such a short acquaintance, yet she saw how silly this was. After all, she hadn't known Vin long before falling under his spell. Tears filled her eyes and impulsively she went to press her mouth to Kevin's cheek. Swiftly his head turned and their lips met, hers trembling, his warm and firm.

From then on, Tansy lost track of the evening. She must have chosen her food and she must have eaten it, and she certainly danced with Kevin. But it wasn't until she found herself on the floor with Vin's arms around her, and the heady scent of him in her nostrils, that she came truly alive: alive to the knowledge that she had irrevocably given her heart to him, and, regardless of whom she met, he would always remain the love of her life.

'You've found yourself a very nice man,' he said quietly.

'I'm aware of that.'

'A pity you didn't tell me about him earlier.'

'I didn't think we'd ever get together again.'

'No man would be stupid enough to let you get away from him.'

Tansy's heart leapt into her throat, and she lowered her head, afraid he would see the pulse beating there. He said no more and neither did she, and, glancing at him from beneath her lashes, she saw his face was calm and relaxed. But his next question warned her to be wary of him.

'Why were you so startled when you saw me without my glasses?'

She thought quickly, then plumped for the truth. She was already involved in too many lies! 'I'd assumed you were Thai.'

He stumbled. 'You didn't know I wasn't?'

'Why should I have? Ever since we met, your face has been half hidden, apart from which you referred to Mr and Mrs Makram as your parents.'

'That's how I regard them.'

'I assumed they really *were*.'

'I see.'

The tempo of the music changed, becoming more languorous, and Vin's arms tightened around her. The blood pounded in her veins as she heard the steady beat of his heart, and she recalled how fast it had pounded when he had lain close beside her. Afraid of giving herself away, she eased back slightly, and he instantly relaxed his hold on her.

'If you'd seen me without my glasses when you first came to Chiang Mai,' he asked abruptly, 'would I have stood a chance with you?'

Caught unawares, Tansy could only stare at him. Then, as her wits returned, she used her hesitation to her advantage.

'That's such a peculiar question, Vin, that it took me a minute to fathom it. Of course it wouldn't have made any difference. Why, I'd love Kevin no matter what nationality he was. And if there'd been the right chemistry between *us*, the same thing would have applied. But there wasn't, and that's the end of it.' She tried a smile. It wobbled but held firm, and she widened it. 'You're a marvellous catch, Vin, and handsome with it, but I guess I prefer blonds!'

His chuckle was one of definite amusement. 'You've well and truly put me in my place. What say we return to the table? I'm sorely in need of a blonde of my own!'

Head high, Tansy preceded him, a picture of grace and beauty that gave no clue to the emptiness inside her.

CHAPTER FIFTEEN

KEVIN didn't return to Australia for another three days, during which time he saw Tansy whenever she was free. She warned him not to expect their pseudo engagement to become real, and though he reassured her he wasn't, she didn't believe him.

Playing the part of the loving fiancée, she saw him off at the airport, and as the plane lifted into the sky she felt more alone than at any time in her life.

Work helped her get through the long days, and tiredness enabled her to sleep fitfully through the long nights. She saw Vin rarely, for he was constantly flying between Chiang Mai and Phuket, but seeing him or not made little difference, for he was in her thoughts whenever she relaxed her guard.

Production at the factory was keeping pace with the orders, and Tansy found it thrilling to see many of her clothes featured in *Vogue* and *Harpers*, and see her name mentioned as the newest star in the fashion firmament.

The only irritating fly in the ointment was the daily presence of Ella at the factory, examining the garments, talking to the workers and constantly calling for Deng's attention.

'Any idea when she's going back to the States?' Tansy asked him late one afternoon as she prepared to leave the office.

'I don't think she is—except for a few weeks to see her father. My impression is that she'll soon be marrying Khun Vin.'

Tansy's bag slipped from her hand and she bent to retrieve it. 'I didn't see him as being interested in marriage. He's more the type for an affair.'

'It may have started out as such, but with a woman as determined as Ella...'

Feigning a yawn, Tansy went to the door, and Deng eyed her with concern. 'When are you going to go on vacation? You look tired.'

'A euphemism for my looking a hag?' she teased.

'A very beautiful one,' he joked back, then grew serious. 'You're too thin and there are shadows beneath your eyes. You are missing Kevin, no?'

'No,' she said without thinking, then instantly corrected herself. 'No more than usual, I mean. But I miss my family and friends too.'

'Then go see them.'

'Kevin would be livid if I bypassed Australia.'

'Go to both! You can afford it.'

'Financially, yes. It's time I'm short of. Nor can I face the emotional upheaval of saying goodbye to them again. Once away from here, I might not return!'

'You aren't serious?' Deng's almond eyes narrowed.

'How can I be when I'm under contract?' she parried. 'Besides, I'd be a fool to walk out when I'm beginning to make a name for myself.'

'Very foolish,' he concurred, accompanying her to the door. 'Let me drive you home.'

Tansy knew better than to argue, and took her place in his car. They chatted idly during the journey, and, arriving at her house, she invited him in for a drink.

Depositing his shoes at the front door, he followed her into the living-room.

'I'll tell Ampa we're here,' she murmured and, shoes in hand, popped into the kitchen before going into her bedroom for a pair of black velvet slippers. 'I can't get used to walking round in bare feet,' she explained as she came out.

'It's habit,' he shrugged. 'I've done it all my life.'

'I suppose if you're brought up to it . . .' She hesitated. She had resisted bringing Vin into the conversation, but a burning urge to learn more of his background now impelled her. 'It's amazing how well Vin fits in here. If it weren't for his eyes he'd pass for Thai.'

'His colouring comes from his Spanish ancestors. A pirate, I think.'

'That figures,' she joked, to keep the atmosphere light. 'What happened to his real parents?'

'His father died saving two Makram daughters from a blazing car—the mother a year later of a broken heart. Vin was four at the time.'

Tansy was shocked. Despising Vin though she did, her heart went out to the little boy left alone.

'Vin was too young to remember them,' Deng went on. 'As far as he's concerned, the Makrams are his parents and he the son they never had.'

'Didn't his real parents have families?' Tansy pressed.

'His father was an orphan, and his mother's family disinherited her when she married.'

'Why were they against it?'

'The man was an artist, and anti blood sports! Hard to credit, eh?' Deng said cheerfully, clearly unmoved by the sorry tale he was recounting. 'Apparently they came to the Far East because it was cheaper to live here, and opened a small art school. After Khun Vin's father died, his mother closed it, and then had some kind of breakdown. The Makrams took care of her, and when she was dying a year later they offered to take her child to his grandparents. She didn't want them to, and they asked her if they could adopt him. The Makrams went on to have five more daughters but never a son, and they see Vin as a gift from God.'

'It's understandable,' Tansy murmured, and appreciated why Mr Makram was anxious for Vin to marry a Thai, for it would bind him here more strongly. 'When did Vin learn the truth?' she asked, careful to keep her voice casual.

'When he was twelve. It was what his real mother wanted. Vin was taken to England to meet his grandparents and finally went to school there. But he refused to live there permanently.'

'I'm glad you told me this,' Tansy said. 'It explains his devotion to the Makrams.'

Deng's large white teeth flashed in a grin. 'Most Thais are devoted to their parents. It's normal behaviour here!'

'I wish it were the same in the West. We can learn a lot from your country.'

Ampa padded in with the chilled white wine and a plate of beautifully presented canapés, and Tansy signalled Deng to help himself.

'We're not only close to our parents,' he said, glass in hand, 'but to all our relatives. That's what I missed most when I lived in the States.'

'But you were with your uncle, weren't you?'

'One uncle and aunt couldn't compensate for the eight I'd left behind!'

Tansy chuckled, and from then on their conversation became general, with Deng showing a keen awareness of world affairs, and refusing to let her discuss anything to do with Arunila.

After he had gone, she had a light meal and went to bed, wakeful for hours as she mulled over Vin's background and the complexity of his character. She

still despised him for the way he had used Ella, and
had tried to use *her*, yet she was petrified in case her
new-found sympathy for him weakened her resolve to
steer clear of him, and knew it was more imperative
than ever to maintain the illusion of her engagement
to Kevin.

She glanced at the ruby ring on her finger, worn to
show Vin she was spoken for, and dreaded the day
when Kevin fell for some other girl, and she could no
longer hide behind its safety. What would she do then?
The question nagged at her for hours and, as always
when personal worries were uppermost, she reached
for her sketch-book. Work was her safety-valve—even
at one in the morning!

To Tansy's relief, Vin remained absent most of the
month, and at the end of it flew to Sydney for another
conference with Jefferson's.

The first batch of clothes left the factory and, with
production well ahead of schedule, Tansy told Deng
to revert to working one shift.

'It's a shame to lose our extra workforce,' he
argued. 'I had a lot of trouble training them in your
ways.'

'I realise that, but we can't carry a hundred extra
women, and we won't be needing them until next
season.'

'Their wages are negligible compared with our
profits.'

'It's still a waste of money.'

With a murmur of acquiescence he went out, but
the sharpness with which he closed the door told her
she should have made her order into a suggestion.
She had taken it for granted that Deng, having worked
for years in the States, was used to Western behaviour, but it seemed he needed to be treated with

the same kid gloves as everyone else here. Customs ingrained since childhood obviously died hard.

The clicking of heels announced Ella's arrival, and she almost bounced into the office, animated with pleasure. 'I'm so happy; Vin's due back today. If I'd known he was going to be away so long I'd have joined him in Sydney.'

Alarmed by her own pleasure at the prospect of seeing him, Tansy hid her face by rummaging in her desk drawer.

'Did I tell you I'm moving into a house?' Ella's question brought Tansy upright.

'No. Any special reason?'

'I'm tired of living in an apartment, and anyway, Vin prefers a house.'

'I can't imagine him having the time to enjoy it!'

'You'd be surprised. It's hard visualising him as a home bird, but he is. He's not a bit like my father. *He's* in his office night and day. But Vin likes to keep family and business apart, and once he leaves the office he switches off completely. I hope to God Dad doesn't change him.'

'How could he?'

'He's decided to invest in some of Vin's projects, so they'll be seeing more of each other, and bad habits are quickly learned!'

Tansy moistened dry lips. 'I'm afraid I'm a workaholic too, so I'd better be quiet!'

'You might take it more easy if Kevin were around!'

'Probably,' Tansy murmured, relieved when Ella, having imparted her news, drifted out in a cloud of Giorgio.

Next morning—anticipating Vin's coming to the factory—Tansy made-up with care, intent on hiding the shadows beneath her eyes and the hollows below her cheekbones. The uncluttered lines of her mint-green dress too clearly showed the weight she had lost these past weeks, and she removed it in favour of a full-skirted cotton in the same colour.

She was touring the factory floor on her daily inspection when she sensed rather than heard Vin's arrival and, carefully turning her head, watched him mount the stairs to her office. The barest glimpse of his tall, lean frame jarred through her like an electric shock, and, knowing he had come to see her, she hurried after him.

He was leaning negligently against the window when she came in, and his greeting was as casual as if they had met yesterday, as was her answering 'hello'.

With the light behind him, she didn't have a clear picture of his face, but as he straightened and moved slightly his silver-grey eyes pierced hers. Would she ever get used to seeing him without his dark glasses, or would she always experience this stab to the heart?

On trembling legs she went to her desk and, using it as a barrier between them, felt able to cope with his presence.

'Had a good trip, Vin?'

'Yes, but a tiring one.'

'How's the shopping mall going?'

'Which one? We're doing four.'

'The one causing the biggest headache!'

'We're headache-free at the moment, I'm pleased to say.'

'I expect you're pleased for other reasons too,' she said drily.

'Oh?' An eyebrow lifted.

'Ella told me her father's going to invest in some of your projects. Being her lover is paying off for you!'

'So it seems.' Vin remained relaxed, one hand in the pocket of his jacket. 'You haven't asked me how Kevin is,' he said softly.

Tansy could have kicked herself. 'I don't have to,' she retorted. 'I speak to him most days.' She hoped Kevin hadn't said anything to give the lie to this, and Vin's silence set her at ease. 'We're well ahead with our orders,' she went on, anxious to put the conversation on a business level. 'If you'd like to look round the factory, I——'

'You're thinner,' he interrupted her.

'You must have been speaking to Deng!'

'Paler too. I take it you're missing Kevin?'

'Naturally. The telephone isn't a satisfactory substitute.'

'He's missing you, too.'

Tansy lowered her head, wishing it were possible to squeeze out a few tears. 'Don't make me feel worse than I already do. If we hadn't had that ridiculous quarrel—which was my own stupid fault—I'd never have signed my contract with you.'

'I'd hardly call it a ridiculous quarrel.' Vin's voice was dry as desert sand. 'From what you told me, you turned him down because he wanted you to travel with him, and you put your career first.'

'If that isn't ridiculous, what is?' Tansy fired back. 'My career's still important—I won't deny it—but it's no longer the be all and end all of my life. If I had the same choice facing me today, I'd put Kevin first.'

Vin's mouth curled with faint derision. 'That's easy to say when you know you won't be called on to do it. Kevin hardly travels since he took over from his father, so he'd be more than happy to give you your own couture house in Sydney.'

The implied insult in his words made her catch her breath. 'Don't judge everyone by your standards. Because your relationship with Ella is expedient——'

'Not altogether. She's very desirable.'

'So is Kevin!' Tansy stopped, furious with herself for entering into this ridiculous slanging match. 'Let's not quarrel, Vin. I'll complete my contract and——'

'That's what I came here to talk about,' he interjected. 'Kevin hasn't been gone two months and you're already a pale ghost. It won't do, Tansy. I knew it when I was in Sydney and I've had it confirmed today.' Silvery eyes raked her. 'The factory's running smoothly, as you say, and even *you* can't fault the finish on the garments. So on that score it's no longer necessary for you to be here. If you carry on designing for us, and come back to supervise the samples, I'm prepared to let you leave Thailand.'

Stunned, Tansy heard him out. She should be overjoyed; after all, this was what she wanted. Yet not to see Vin again ... Desolation swamped her. It was as if a black shroud had enveloped her, blotting out sunlight, warmth, happiness. With freedom facing her, she knew she was going into a prison of her own making.

Hard on these thoughts came the fear of his reaction when he discovered she'd gone to England and not Australia. He'd think her mad! Unless she stayed in Sydney several months and then pretended she and Kevin had broken up again.

Vin's movement as he went to the door brought her to her feet. 'Isn't there anything else for us to discuss?' she asked.

Silver eyes held a mocking glint as they surveyed her. 'What else is there—other than for me to accept defeat gracefully?'

'Hardly defeat. I'll still be with Arunila.'

'But not with me!'

Angrily she swung away. 'What a swine you are! I'm tempted to tell Ella.'

'Don't you dare!' In two strides he was beside her, fingers clamped on her forearm. 'If you breathe a word to her, I'll hold you to the letter of our contract. Is that clear? Not a damn word!'

Contemptuously Tansy stared into his set face. My God, he was really scared!

'You're unbelievable, Vin. You're rich beyond dreams, yet you're willing to prostitute yourself! And you know something? Your father couldn't care less about keeping Arunila going! The only reason he pretended he did was to keep you in Chiang Mai.'

'I'm aware of that,' came the quiet answer.

'You are?' Tansy was shocked. 'Yet you still...' She couldn't go on, finding it too painful. Yet, pain or not, she had to know the truth. 'You're with Ella because you *want* to be. What you said to me about letting her down lightly was just talk, wasn't it? You had no intention of leaving her for me!'

Impassively Vin regarded her, then with a lift of his shoulders he went to the door.

'Vin! Have you nothing to say?'

Turning, he regarded her again. But this time he spoke. 'Call Kevin and tell him your good news. He deserves to have a nice day.'

The door opened and closed, and Tansy sank on to her chair and buried her head in her hands, mourning for a man who had never existed, and a happiness that could never be hers.

CHAPTER SIXTEEN

KEVIN gave a shout of laughter when he learned Vin had agreed to let Tansy work from Sydney.

'That's great, sweetheart! Best news I've had in weeks. Aren't you jumping over the moon?'

'Not quite. Vin will expect me to stay in Australia with you.'

'What's wrong with that? It's a great city and a great country—and I'm a great guy!'

'All true. But it isn't my home.'

'Neither is Thailand, but you'd have remained there permanently if things had worked out for you and Vin.'

'That was different.'

Kevin said a rude word, then hastily apologised. 'You're worrying for nothing. Come here for six months and go back to England after that, if you still want to. Vin won't be keeping tabs on us, and when he asks how you are I'll say "fine".'

Kevin's suggestion was logical, and if she weren't emotionally mixed up she'd have reached the same conclusion.

With his confident voice ringing in her ears, she went home. Tomorrow was soon enough to tell Deng her news, and they would have to evolve a plan of operation. Designing from a distance was not as simple as Vin assumed, and her visits back here weren't likely to be as brief as he imagined. But it was better than staying here full time.

Though Vin had said he was letting her go because he was concerned for her, on reflection she doubted it. More likely he was running scared that she'd put Ella wise as to the kind of man he was. Yet, whatever his reasons, she was free to leave.

With her departure imminent, she eyed Chiang Mai with more than her usual affection, and wondered if Vin would think it odd if she elected to travel round Thailand for a month before going to Australia. Amazing to think she could contemplate this when only a few months ago her financial future had been bleak.

Today she had an excellent salary, fantastic bonuses geared to profits, and a chance to become famous worldwide. It was a glorious future, yet because she had fallen in love with the wrong man it meant little to her.

Entering Tom and Siri's house—pity she'd never see them—she showered and changed into trousers and sweater—more suitable to the cooler evenings—then sat on the porch overlooking the garden.

At ten o'clock, unexpectedly tired, she went to bed, and awoke at midnight as refreshed as if she had slept the night through. She thrashed around, courting sleep with little success, and finally padded into the kitchen to make herself a hot chocolate.

It was pointless returning to bed—she was wider awake than ever—and she might as well go to the factory and start clearing out her desk. It beat staying here, feeling miserable as hell!

The streets were deserted at this hour, and in next to no time she was deposited at the gates let into the high wall which surrounded the two factories. She peered through the bars for sight of a security guard.

None was in sight, and she fished in her bag for the key to open a small door further down the wall.

Once inside, she hurried across the compound. The entrance to the factory was dimly lit, yet sufficient for her to see her way across the foyer and up the stairs.

Reaching the first floor, she noticed that the fire door leading to the main sewing-room was closed. Until now she had always seen it open, and she wondered if it was shut for safety reasons. As she paused, she became aware of a shaft of light seeping from beneath it. Strange! They were only doing day shifts now, and no one bar herself came in at night. Puzzled, she climbed to the second floor. The fire door was closed here too, and again light seeped from beneath it.

Pushing it open, she stopped dead as she heard the murmur of voices. Thieves! She was poised to rush down and alert the guards when she heard Deng's voice. She heaved a sigh of relief, suddenly conscious she was trembling. It served to show the power of an overworked imagination!

She continued along the corridor to her office, her track shoes making no sound. Deng's voice was still audible but there were other voices too, female ones. Maybe he had asked a few seamstresses to work late and clear the backlog.

Yet there wasn't any backlog. According to Deng they were ahead of schedule. Curious to see what was going on, she headed for the main workroom.

A hive of activity met her eyes. Only a few seamstresses! Why, there were dozens here, all snipping and sewing, with Deng moving down the aisles, pausing occasionally to examine a garment.

What the hell was going on?

Frowning, she advanced into the room. A woman noticed her and tugged at Deng's arm. He swung round and, seeing Tansy, hurried over.

'This is an unexpected visit,' he greeted her.

'I was restless and came back to clear my desk. What's going on?'

'When I was double checking the shipment we're sending Impo, I noticed some rough seams and badly fitted shoulder-pads, so I asked a few girls to come in tonight and redo them.'

'Show me.' Tansy headed for the nearest girl, and saw her nimbly adjusting a pad.

'Don't bother yourself with it,' Deng enjoined. 'These are *my* worries, not yours.'

'Anything connected with the clothes is my problem too,' she reminded him.

'Don't you have confidence in me?'

'You can't be serious!'

Pleased by this, he guided her to the door. 'When you're ready to leave I'll drive you home.'

'I'm not sure how long I'll be.'

'I'll come back in half an hour and see.'

In her office, she was too restless to do what she had come here for, and, strangely uneasy, she paced the floor. She had made a point of talking to most of the girls in the factory, yet tonight she had not recognised any of them. Her uneasiness grew. Was there more wrong with the garments than Deng had admitted? And had he brought in skilled dressmakers to put things right?

Determined to find out, she returned to the workroom. Anxious not to be seen by Deng—who would think she didn't trust his judgement—she bent low and kept behind a row of packing cases to survey the scene.

A few yards ahead, two tables were stacked with clothes and, as she watched, several girls approached the first table to remove a bundle of them, returning some ten minutes later to place them on the second table.

Intent on seeing both the altered and unaltered clothing, Tansy inched forward, but despite her care her movement caught the eye of one of the girls. Quickly Tansy gave her a conspiratorial wink and put her finger to her lips. The girl nodded and resumed stitching, leaving Tansy free to remove two dresses from each pile before hurrying out.

In her office she carefully examined them. There didn't appear to be anything wrong with the two waiting to be altered, but the ones which had been redone were dreadful. She had never seen shoulder-pads sewn in so badly! Could she have muddled up the dresses and be looking at two garments that *hadn't* been fixed?

Closing her eyes, she went back over her actions. No, the altered dresses had been on the left table, and these were the ones she was holding. How in heaven's name had Deng passed such work? Loss of face or not, she'd give him a rocket!

Reaching for her scissors, she snipped out the ill-fitting pads. They seemed unusually heavy, and she checked them against a pad in an unaltered garment.

The unaltered pad weighed less. Puzzled, she un-picked the material covering a heavier pad. As the fabric came away she peered at the moulded foam. Odd. The thickest part of it had been slit. Carefully she prised the slit open.

Oh, no! She was dreaming. It couldn't be true. Yet it was. Terribly, horribly true.

Grimly she extracted the small plastic packet of white powder which had been inserted into the slit. No marks for guessing it was heroin!

Collapsing into her chair, she let the package slip from her fingers. Only one explanation was possible, and it made clear many things which had puzzled her about Deng: his willingness to accept her without jealousy when he himself was a dress designer; his readiness to remain as a factory manager; the inordinately long hours he worked at night without complaining.

Unbelievable though it was, he was a drug dealer!

For an instant she was too paralysed by shock to think straight. Then her brain started functioning, and she lifted the receiver to call the police. Damn! There was no outside line and the switchboard was closed. She'd have to call from home.

Bundling the dresses and pads into a drawer, she put the packet of heroin into her bag and went to the door. Opening it, she came face to face with Deng.

'Oh!' Her heart leapt into her throat. 'You startled me,' she said in a falsely bright voice. 'I was coming to find you. I'll have that lift home after all.'

'You will?'

'If you aren't too busy, that is.' She essayed another smile, but it wobbled badly as she saw the greyness of his skin.

'A good try, Tansy, but it won't work.' Deng's voice was high, and barely recognisable as the one she knew.

'A good try?' she echoed. 'I don't follow you.'

For answer, he pulled her back into the office, and she swore silently as she saw she had left a piece of fabric on the desk. Clutching her, Deng dragged her over to the desk and flung open the drawers until he found the dresses.

'I'm sorry you came here tonight,' he grunted. 'And don't pretend you don't know what's going on, because you're too bright not to.'

'Why are you doing it?' she asked. 'You don't need the money. You're well paid and——'

'Well paid, when I can have millions? Enough to start my own company.'

'Is that what this is about? Bringing misery and death to thousands of people so you can have your own business?'

He glared at her, his eyes narrowed. She didn't know what he planned to do with her, but she sensed she was in mortal danger. Yet she couldn't stay silent, waiting for the sword to fall; she had to make a fight of it.

'Don't go on with this, Deng. Give it up. If you do, I'll forget everything I've seen here tonight. I give you my word.'

'Don't be naïve. You think I can stop, just like that? Suspend delivery and wave goodbye?' His face was ugly with rage, and fear too. 'I'm in too deep to pull out now. If I tried, I'd be killed. It's you or me, Tansy, and that leaves me no choice.'

'You can't murder me!'

'I'm sorry.'

She began to shake: her body, her voice, every single part of her. 'I'll keep quiet, Deng. I swear I will. Let me go and I won't tell a soul. I'm leaving the country anyway, and——'

'Don't play me for a fool! You'll go to the police the moment I let you go.'

Recognising the futility of arguing, she didn't bother trying. She had to concentrate on escaping. That was her number one priority.

'How are you g-going to kill me?' she asked shakily.

'You'll have an accident. You weren't able to get a taxi home and decided to walk until you found one. You stepped out into the street without seeing a car coming, and...' He shrugged off the rest.

'You'll never get away with it,' Tansy derided, but knew he would. It was a simple plan and easy to execute. Her shaking intensified. What a way for her life to end. Splattered on a road thousands of miles from her family, her country, from anyone who genuinely cared for her.

'What have you done with it?' Deng snarled.

'With what?'

'The packet that was in one of the pads.'

Mutely she regarded him and his fingers bit into her flesh, the pressure increasing until she gave a cry of pain. 'It's in my bag,' she gasped.

Fumbling it open, he extracted it and slipped it into his pocket. Then he handed her the bag and dragged her into the corridor.

'Are the girls in on this too?' she asked.

'Only the ones who are putting the packets into the pads.'

That meant half the women here tonight were innocent. If she could attract the attention of one of them... Hardly had the notion entered her head when cold steel pressed into her side.

'One cry and I'll twist the knife,' Deng warned.

With the point of the blade digging into her skin, Tansy saw little hope of saving herself. If she screamed, he'd stab her long before a security guard came to her aid. Besides, they might be in league with him. On trembling legs she stumbled along the corridor and, as they reached the stairs, Ella came running up them, smiling.

'Get out!' Tansy screamed. 'Run for it, Ella! Deng will kill you!'

But Ella kept on running and kept on smiling. Tansy went cold as ice. Ella was in on this too! Horrified, she stared into the beautiful face, marvelling that it held no sign of evil.

'You're in league with Deng!'

'No, honey. He's in league with *me*.'

Shock held Tansy rigid. Ella was controlling this operation! Or was she? Could a female reach such a position in a business that was dominated by men? One possible answer came to her.

Vin. *He* was the mastermind.

Suddenly everything slotted into place. His knowledge of the hill tribes and northern Thailand, where the heroin was smuggled across the borders; his frequent journeys around the world—to check his pushers, no doubt—and, most damning of all, his unwillingness to end his affair with Ella, despite admitting he loved *her*.

Recalling his condemnation of drug smuggling, she awarded him top marks for acting. His perfidy and greed disgusted her. As head of a property empire he had money enough to satisfy his most ambitious dreams. Or had drug money created his empire in the first place?

'What are you going to do with her?' Ella asked Deng.

'A hit-and-run accident.'

'Be careful she doesn't run for cover before she's knocked down.'

'Don't worry. We'll untie her legs *after* she's dead.'

Ella smoothed a strand of blonde hair. 'Use one of the other men's cars, not yours.'

'I'd already thought of that.'

'And come straight back. We're running late.' Only then did Ella favour Tansy with another glance. 'Seems as if Vin will have to find another designer. Pity about that. You were fantastic!'

'You rotten bitch!'

'At least I'm not a dead one!'

Laughing at her little joke, Ella hurried off, and Tansy was dragged down to the ground floor and out into the compound. Two security guards by the main door watched impassively as Deng pushed her towards one of the cars.

Tansy clenched her hands at her sides. Damn them to hell! If she was going to die she'd make a fight of it. They'd have to knife her to silence her, and how would they explain her death then?

She tensed her muscles, ready to run, and in that instant saw Vin come round the side of the building. She'd been right about him! The pain of it was so intense it almost made her accept her inevitable death. Almost, but not quite. Giving Deng a violent push, she raced towards the gates.

Deng shouted to the guards and they charged after her. As they did, floodlights blazed into life, illuminating the entire area. Police swarmed from everywhere, encircling Deng and the guards, storming into the factory, heading for the parked cars, and in the centre of the mêlée was Vin, fighting for his life.

I can't bear it! was Tansy's last thought. Not Vin, not Vin. Then blackness whooshed in on her and she knew no more.

CHAPTER SEVENTEEN

TANSY opened her eyes to find herself lying in the back of a moving car. She heard men talking, and a policeman beside her was holding smelling salts under her nose. As she coughed and sat up, he murmured reassuringly in his own language.

'What happened?' she asked huskily. 'How long have you known about the smuggling? Where are Khun Vin and the others?'

The policeman answered in Thai, and frustratedly she stared through the window, relieved to see they were drawing to a stop outside her house. The man escorted her to the front door, and spoke again. She made out the words *phroong-nee* and *kao mong chao*, and touched her watch to show she understood they would be coming to see her tomorrow morning at nine. Then he saw her safely inside and left her.

Talk about anticlimax! Tansy entered the living-room and dissolved into tears. She had never expected to see this room again, and, though thankful to be alive, she knew the events of tonight would haunt her for ever.

Longing to talk to someone who spoke English, she stumbled towards Ampa's room, then stopped as she remembered the woman was spending the night at her daughter's home.

Agitatedly she paced the floor, still shattered by her narrow escape from death, but even more shattered by Vin's culpability. With so much going for him, how could he have succumbed to such evil? In the midst

178

of her pain, she suffered for his adoptive parents too. What a tragedy this was for them!

The urge to talk it out impelled her to the telephone. Who should she call? Her parents and sister didn't know Vin, or how she felt about him, and she was too overwrought to go into explanations. That left only Kevin. He was the natural person for her to confide in. The mere anticipation of doing so brought tears of relief, and she could hardly see to dial. Damn! She'd forgotten to put in the overseas code.

She was halfway through doing it when there was a rap at the front door.

She whirled round. Who was calling on her at this hour? It wasn't the police, for she was seeing them in the morning. The rap came again, quicker and louder, and her heart thumped in time to it. Was it one of Vin's accomplices, come to kill her? Perhaps they hoped one witness less might help them.

Crouching low, though she knew she couldn't be seen through the curtained window, she went to dial emergency. Except she didn't know the number! Was it 999 as in England? No, every country had its own system. She'd have to call the operator.

'Tansy! Let me in.' It was Vin, his voice hard, urgent.

Petrified, she stood rooted to the spot. He had escaped and had come to kill her himself! The blood drained from her head and the room darkened and began to spin. Digging her nails into the palms of her hands, she fought for consciousness.

'Tansy, let me in,' he demanded. 'I know you're there.'

'I have a gun!' she cried. 'Kevin gave it me for protection. If you break in I'll shoot!'

For answer there was a crash at the door. It splintered, and Tansy screamed and raced to the bedroom. Steps pounded behind her, and iron hands swung her round in mid-flight.

Staring into the darkly intent face, she tried to beg for her life. But the horror of knowing that the man she loved was going to murder her rendered her dumb.

'What is it?' he demanded, shaking her hard.

'D-don't kill me. Don't be a murderer too!'

'*Kill* you?' Fingers dug deep into her flesh. 'Is that why you think I'm here? Oh, God!'

With a groan he pulled her against him. The heat from his body was tangible, and, pressed close to him, she smelled the dust and grime and sweat of hours. Never had she seen him so dishevelled, and never had she loved him more.

'I was working with the *police*,' he said heavily. 'That's why I was at the factory.'

Once again tried to speak but couldn't, and, sensing she was at the end of her tether, he half carried her into the bedroom and placed her on the bed.

'When I saw you going into the factory tonight, I *could* have murdered you,' he said, sitting beside her. 'You gave me a hell of a shock turning up when you did.'

'You saw me arrive?' Tansy found her wits and her tongue. 'Why didn't you stop me going in?'

'The police held me back. I have the bruises to prove it! If I'd come after you it would have blown our cover, and we'd been waiting months to catch everyone red-handed.' He leaned close to her. 'I just prayed that when you were inside you wouldn't tumble to what was going on, but when I saw Deng dragging you out ...' Vin shook his head, as if trying to obliterate the memory. 'What actually went on?'

Briefly Tansy filled him in. 'I tried to persuade Deng I'd forget what I saw,' she concluded, 'but he wasn't having any. If you hadn't been there, I'd be dead by now!'

'And left me with a lot of explaining to do to Kevin!' Vin said in a jokey voice, though the grey tinge to his bronze skin showed he was far from over the shock of the night's events. 'He'd never have forgiven me if anything had happened to you.'

Tansy lowered her lids. Mention of Kevin brought Vin's association with Ella to mind. 'You must have been pretty shattered when you learned Ella was involved with the smuggling,' she murmured.

'I knew it almost from day one.'

'You did?' Tansy sat up straight. 'How?'

'Because of her father. He's been top of Interpol's list for more than two years, but they couldn't pin anything on him. They knew he was bringing the heroin into the States, and distributing it, but they didn't know how. Then last summer Ella approached me and said their company wanted to import and distribute Arunila clothes. I was amazed—as you can imagine!—and I casually mentioned it to a friend of mine. Next thing I knew, Interpol came on the scene and asked me to take up Impo's offer. I wasn't thrilled at being seconded to them—that's what it amounted to—but I couldn't refuse. Then, shortly afterwards, Ella suggested we find a new designer, and the rest is history.'

'Not quite.' As Tansy's shock lessened, her curiosity grew. 'If Impo were only using the clothes to distribute the drugs, what did it matter how awful they were?'

'I knew you'd enjoy rubbing *that* in!' Vin answered drily. 'But if the clothes didn't sell, it would have looked suspicious if Impo continued distributing them. They have warehouses in all the major cities in the States, and when our shipments arrived there the packets would have been removed. Interpol assumed the heroin would be hidden in the crates, but they weren't a hundred per cent sure, and wouldn't make their bust until the first batch of orders was ready for delivery. They asked me to play Ella along until then.'

Tansy was instantly alert, but knew better than to show it.

'Pretending I'd fallen for her was the hardest part of the entire undertaking,' Vin went on. 'I can't make love to order, regardless of how important it is to my plans, and the accident to my eye got me out of a tight corner. I told her I'd been forbidden to have any physical exertion until the damage had healed!'

'A lucky accident, then!'

'If I hadn't had it, I'd have invented it!'

'It's strange you didn't fancy her. She's very lovely.'

'In normal circumstances she might have appealed,' he admitted, 'but suspecting her as I did turned me off.'

Tansy hid her satisfaction. Everything Vin was saying changed the position between herself and him. Of course he had never said he loved *her*—he had only used the word 'want'—but if he still did, was she willing to have an affair with him now she knew he had never had one with Ella?

The answer was yes. She loved him so much she was prepared to accept what he offered. It was storing up anguish for herself in the future, but she'd at least have wonderful memories. She half raised her hand towards him, stopping abruptly as the ruby on her finger glowed in the lamplight.

Vin wouldn't take her while she was engaged to Kevin, and if she admitted the engagement was phoney, he'd guess it had been a ploy to ward him off. Worse still, he might realise she had done it in order to hide the fact that she loved him! And that was something she still intended hiding. Better to let him assume her desire for him was, like his for her, purely physical.

But first she had to end the Kevin episode. Perhaps if he came here for a few weeks and they were seen to quarrel... Yes, that was the best plan. She'd call him the minute Vin left. Excitement made her tremble, and in an effort to control it she concentrated on the happenings of the last hour.

'How did Deng get involved?' she asked.

'Ella met him at a party in California, and, because he was Thai, concluded he'd be useful. I suspect they had an affair and she got him hooked on drugs. She wanted him in our factory, and told him to contact me. Interpol knew the two of them were close, and asked me to engage him.'

'Where do Jefferson's come in?'

'They don't.'

'Then why was Impo investing in your projects with them?'

'Because it's a profitable business, and the more above board Impo could be, the better for them. Don't worry about Kevin. He's straight as a die.'

Vin rose and went to stand by the window. The lamplight was dim, and from this distance Tansy found it hard to read his expression.

'Now you know the truth about Ella and me,' he said casually, 'I hope you'll stop regarding me as a two-timing philanderer!'

'I'll grovel, if it will make you feel better!'

'Forget that! It was my fault for coming on to you so strongly.'

Heart beating like a drum, she waited for him to elaborate, but when he spoke she nearly screamed with frustration.

'When are you leaving for Australia, Tansy?'

'I haven't decided. Without Deng in the factory I'll need to supervise production. It won't be easy getting anyone as good.'

'I already have a man in mind.'

The crisp statement floored her hopes of staying here long enough to put her plan about Kevin into action, and she was debating what to do when Vin spoke again.

'You may leave as soon as you wish. My main concern is your happiness.'

This was getting worse and worse, and her only option was to grasp the nettle. 'I'm not sure I—er—want to marry Kevin. We rather rushed into our engagement, and I think I . . . I'd like longer to get to know him.'

'You'll feel differently when you see him again.'

How eager he was to have her go! She averted her face in case he saw the hurt on it. 'There's my career too. If I'm in Sydney, Kevin will demand my attention, and it will be impossible to concentrate on him *and* my work.'

'I see. In that case, I'll arrange for you to return to England.'

Expecting Vin to jump at the chance of her remaining here, she was flummoxed for a reply. 'If that's what you wish,' she said stiffly.

For a long moment there was silence. He remained by the window, arms folded across his chest, neither his stance nor expression indicating his thoughts. She longed to admit she loved him but was afraid of rejection. Only a matter of hours ago he had made it clear he still wanted her, yet now he didn't seem to. Perhaps being free of Ella and the whole drug situation had made him decide to put everyone connected with the episode out of his life. In a way it was understandable. He'd have to see her from time to time to discuss the various collections, but apart from that there was no reason for their paths to cross.

'As soon as Deng's replacement arrives,' she said, 'I'll leave.'

'Very well.' His arms dropped to his sides. 'It's interesting how things work out. When Impo erupted into my life, I was preparing to close Arunila. It was more bother than it was worth, and I knew my father's sentimentality about it was only a means of keeping me here. Now Impo and all it stood for is gone, and I've also managed to convince my parents they won't be losing me to the delights of the West. Yet I can't close Arunila because it looks like becoming one of the biggest money spinners in my empire!'

'You don't sound too pleased about it,' Tansy commented, aware of the bitter irony in his voice. 'I thought you liked success.'

'Not when it destroys my peace of mind.'

'Arunila shouldn't do that. If Deng's replacement is no good, I'll stay until I find someone else. If we offer enough money we'll get the right person.'

'I hope to God you don't!'

'Vin!'

'I'm sorry. I shouldn't have said that, but ...' He strode to the side of the bed and peered down at her. 'Don't go to England, Tansy. Work from here. If you do, I swear I'll keep our relationship strictly businesslike.'

Tansy's heart raced like a piston but she kept her voice flat. 'Can I assume you won't be propositioning me again?'

'Yes. You have my solemn promise.'

'In that case I won't stay.'

Mystified, he stared at her, then he gave a deep growl and stooped low to gather her close, rocking her backwards and forwards in his arms and murmuring broken endearments.

'Darling...dearest...I need you so much...you're everything I've dreamed of. If it hadn't been for this drug business, I'd have asked you to marry me months ago. I know I'm rushing you, but you have to know how I feel.'

'Marry you?' Tansy pushed him slightly away from her so she could see his face. 'Did you say marry?'

'What else?'

What else indeed? If happiness had wings, hers would be strong enough to fly her to the moon!

'Will you?' he demanded. 'I know you thought me a bastard for wanting you, yet refusing to give up Ella, but I was so scared you'd fall for someone else, I had to tell you how I felt.'

'You could have been a little less obscure. *I* felt you wanted a bit extra on the side!'

'I know. And I could have kicked myself for not keeping quiet a bit longer, except as I said I was scared of losing you. Then when Kevin came on the scene and announced your engagement, I hit rock-bottom.'

'*I'd* been at rock-bottom for weeks,' Tansy confessed. 'I think I fell in love with you that day we spent together in Bangkok.'

'That's when it began for me, too,' he said thickly, and, pressing her back upon the pillows, lay down beside her. 'Will you be happy making your life here with me? Emotionally, this is my home.'

'I know. Deng told me the whole story.'

'I've an estate in Cornwall,' he added. 'My grandparents left it to me, and I have aunts and a host of cousins there with whom I get on well. But as long as my "parents" are alive, this is where I'll remain.'

'They were hoping you'd marry a Thai,' Tansy couldn't help saying.

'As soon as they saw the way I looked at you, they knew I wouldn't. And they were drawn to you, darling, and are ready to welcome you as their daughter.'

Tears of joy shimmered in her eyes, and she touched the side of Vin's face, loving the high sweep of his forehead, the slightly long nose, the incisive mouth and jaw. 'My life is where *you* are, Vin, though I can't become a Buddhist.'

'I wouldn't ask you to. Anyway, I follow the religion of my blood parents.' He lowered his lips to the soft curve of her throat. 'I know we have much to talk over, but at the moment there are other things more pressing.'

'Such as?'

'I'll give you three guesses.'

She laughed, the sound dying in her throat as his mouth covered hers, and his tongue parted her lips to drain the sweetness within. A tremor racked him and his kiss deepened and grew more demanding, until Tansy felt her soul were being drawn from her and given into his keeping.

'I love you,' he whispered, his breath mingling with hers.

'Tell me more.'

'I'd rather show you.'

The tip of his tongue traced the curve of her cheek, while his hands eased off her sweater and found the soft swell of her breasts. His lips fastened on a soft pink nub, sucking it hard and sending a shaft of desire piercing through her. Her cries of pleasure aroused him more, and she was achingly conscious of the throbbing muscle pressing upon her thigh. Her need of him, stifled for months, broke free, and she arched towards him, her parted mouth an invitation.

'This isn't the safest place to plight our troth,' he warned, silver-grey eyes looking deep into hers. 'This bed is giving me too many ideas.'

'Is that so?' Winding her arms around him, she rubbed her leg against his. 'I like a man with imagination!'